About the Storyweaver series . . .

These true stories will not only open your children's eyes to how God is defending orphans around the world, but will also show how he provides for them today through the obedience of Christ's disciples, young and old.

—*Rick Carter, HGBC Missions Coordinator, Northern KY*

I love this book because it has true stories about real kids who need families and love and don't have what most kids do.

—Chelsie Voge, age ten

My son and I read *Tales of the Not Forgotten* together, and it really challenged us in the way we think about our world. It encouraged us to talk about poverty, suffering, the call of the gospel, and our response to the Great Commission. I'm so thankful for the discussion times he and I had as a result of reading this book together.

—*Matt Markins, D6 Conference Cofounder*

POST CARD

CORRESPONDENCE

I read *Tales of the Not Forgotten* on a flight and tried not to make a scene as I constantly fought back the tears. . . . Since then, any time I'm in a conversation about helping kids develop a heart that breaks for what breaks our Lord's heart, this book is the first thing I mention.

—*Tina Houser, Publications Director, KidzMatter, Inc.*

Beth captures not only the harsh realities of life for children all over the world, but also how they intersect with beautiful stories of God using his people to live out the gospel—all written in a voice ideal for preteen kids. These stories have much potential for mobilizing this generation to make a difference in the world.

—*Jenny Funderburke, Minister to Children,*
West Bradenton Baptist Church

Tales of the Not Forgotten is a masterfully woven book. Beth in her patented story-telling style connects you to the cry of the orphan throughout the world. . . . My daughter now understands better what it mean to "look after orphans and widows."

—*Curtis Cecil, father of six, two adopted*

Beth is one of the most anointed ministers of the gospel I know. Her powerful storytelling leaves you—and your preteens—feeling emboldened to take part in how God is moving in the world.

—*Evan Doyle, Communication Specialist,*
KidzMatter, Inc.

One of the highlights of my year was getting to know Beth and to get to see and hear her heart for God and his kids around the world. I'm excited about this new book and how God is defending the orphan. Make sure you read *Tales of the Not Forgotten*—it's a game changer!

—*Jim Wideman, children's ministry pioneer,*
Jim Wideman Ministries

This book changed my daughter's life—she was brought to tears reading the stories of the children. Her teacher stated that she can tell this book changed Ceili.

—*Chelle Lynn, reader*

I was truly captivated by *Tales of the Not Forgotten*. Beth places the reader right there beside the characters as they go through their pain and turmoil, and eventually experience the touch of our great Lord's hand. This book tugs at your heart, prompts you to do more, and demonstrates that God will never leave us, nor forsake us (Hebrews 13:5).

—*Amy Tuell, Mission Team Leader*

This book has provided a graspable path for my children to be exposed to the needs of kids around the globe. Together we praise God for what he is doing and ask, how can we help?

—*Krista Regan, mama of two boys who love Jesus*

The Storyweaver series reminds us all that nothing happens by accident. These stories are living proof that every act of kindness is part of God's master plan. They inspire us to look twice, extend a hand, offer a smile—you never know when the Storyweaver will use us to change others' lives, or use them to change ours.

—*Tina Rogal, sponsor mom of kids in Mexico and Africa*

The Storyweaver series helped me to see that the face of Jesus is a child I have never met, in a place I may never go to, hurting in a way I may never be able to fully understand. . . . These stories show just how far the arm of the Lord reaches and just how deep and wide his love is.

—*Melissa Parsons, wife, mother, and servant*

Tales of the Not Forgotten is a must read because it highlights the desperate plight of the orphan around the world through gripping, true stories. 163,000,000 orphans get a voice in this work.

—*James Wendell Bush, Minister to Students,*
Rosemont Baptist Church

Beth is a master storyteller—one of the best there is anywhere in the contemporary church—to which any of the tens-of-thousands who have heard her speak can attest. As cohost of our national radio show, *Real Life, Real Talk*, I have the joy of hearing these stories every week. . . . In *Tales of the Not Forgotten* she transports readers through her personal and heartfelt style into the gripping stories that mark Back2Back's labor of love among orphans and impoverished people around the world. Once I read *Tales* I invariably found myself talking to everyone I knew about the God-sized, compassionate, riveting, and profound stories I found inside.

—*Dr. Rob Hall, Research Analyst,*
Cincinnati Hills Christian Academy

Throughout Scripture we see that God's heart is for the orphans. . . . In a compelling way, Beth moves the open-hearted person from just caring *about* the orphan to becoming a person who will care *for* the orphan. She presents the clear and emotive reality of life as an orphan in such a manner that people rise up to take action for these precious ones.

—*Steve Biondo, SVP, Family Christian Stores,*
President, The James Fund

Beth Guckenberger and her husband Todd have a gift for sharing God's love with the fatherless and the forgotten. . . . They have truly delighted themselves in the Lord and he has given them the desires of their heart. What an example set for us to imitate in our own lives.

—*J.D. Gibbs, president of Joe Gibbs Racing*

Tales of the Not Forgotten has been a great book for our family to read together. We're hearing the stories and being inspired as a family to care more for orphans.

—*Matt Massey, Lead Pastor at Northstar*

After reading these stories, it's difficult to see the world as "out there" instead of "next door" and impossible *not* to want to help more children like these. . . . The *Leader's Guide* is absolutely perfect—it contains everything you would need to turn this book into a series of mission lessons for kids. . . . It's truly perfect for young youth groups, homeschool groups, Sunday school classes, etc. I read many great books, and some stick in my head for a long time afterwards. Some I'm eager to share with my friends and family . . . but never before have I had plans to share a book with so many others within days of turning the last page. As you read this book, you can't help but want to be a part of someone else's story—to have a hand in helping them see that the God of the Universe has not forgotten them.

—*Amy Bradsher, wife and homeschooling mom,*
anestintherocks.blogspot.com

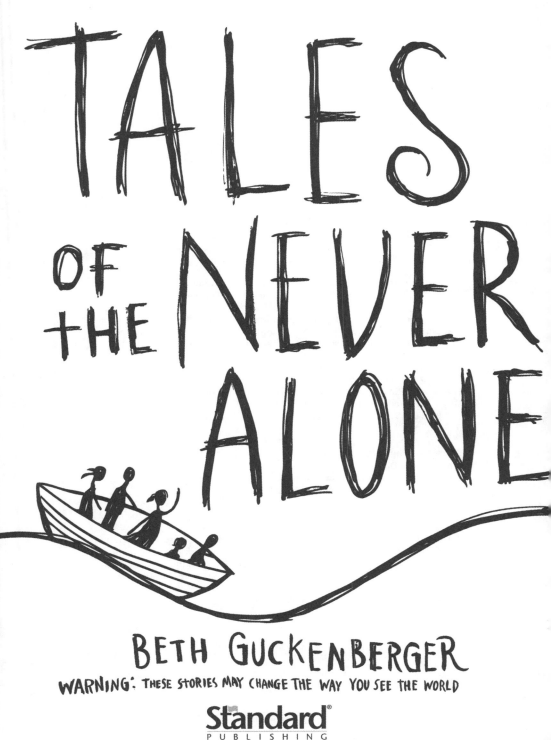

TALES OF THE NEVER ALONE

BETH GUCKENBERGER

WARNING: THESE STORIES MAY CHANGE THE WAY YOU SEE THE WORLD

Standard®
PUBLISHING

Cincinnati, Ohio

Published by Standard Publishing, Cincinnati, Ohio
www.standardpub.com

These stories are inspired by true events and real people. In some cases, names and photos were changed to protect identities and details of dialogue and actions were imagined. Six billion stories are unfolding daily. These are just a few.

Also available: *Tales of the Ones He Won't Let Go*, 978-0-7847-7634-6; *Tales of the Ones Led Out*, 978-0-7847-7522-6; *Tales of the Ones Led Out Leader's Guide*, 978-0-7847-7521-9, *Tales of the Defended Ones*, 978-0-7847-3697-5; *Tales of the Defended Ones Leader's Guide*, 978-0-7847-3698-2; *Tales of the Not Forgotten*, 978-0-7847-3528-2; *Tales of the Not Forgotten Leader's Guide*, 978-0-7847-3527-5.

Printed in: United States of America
Editor: Laura Derico
Cover design and illustration: Scott Ryan
Interior typesetting: Ahaa! Design, Dina Sorn

ISBN 978-0-7847-7769-5

20 19 18 17 16 15   1 2 3 4 5 6 7 8 9

Storyweaver Series by Beth Guckenberger

Tales of the Not Forgotten

Tales of the Not Forgotten Leader's Guide

Tales of the Defended Ones

Tales of the Defended Ones Leader's Guide

Tales of the Ones Led Out

Tales of the Ones Led Out Leader's Guide

Tales of the Ones He Won't Let Go

Tales of the Never Alone

Associated Titles

Kids Serving Kids Mission Kit:

featuring Tales of the Not Forgotten

Kids Serving Kids Mission Kit:

featuring Tales of the Ones He Won't Let Go

Other Titles by Beth Guckenberger

Relentless Hope

Reckless Faith

To Tyler,
Jesus took my breath away when he said we
were family. I will spend the rest of my life
watching all the reasons why. Te quiero.

CONTENTS

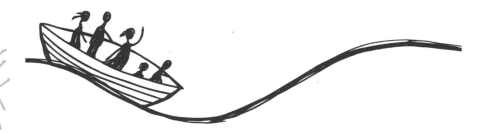

The LORD will keep you from all harm—
he will watch over your life;
the LORD will watch over your coming and going
both now and forevermore.

—Psalm 121:7, 8

INTRODUCTION
THE GUIDE

"The Lord will watch over your coming and going."
—Psalm 121:8

I have always loved the water. I grew up on a lake, and whether I am walking around water, diving into water, or throwing someone into it, water makes me feel at home. As I write this, our family is finishing up an international adoption of a twelve-year-old boy. He grew up in an urban, international setting, without access to a pool, let alone a lake or an ocean. Recently I was able to introduce him to the sea. At first he only wanted to get his ankles wet. The waves were intimidating—relentless and powerful. He asked questions like, "Do they ever stop?" "What makes some smaller and others huge?" "What lives under the water?" "Why is it salty?" They were all good questions, and regardless of his initial fear, he was driven by his curiosity (and my encouragement), and by the end of the first day, we were bodysurfing to shore.

During that process, as we inched each time a bit deeper into the water, he had to learn to trust me. He'd grab my arm, or listen when I said, "Here it comes!" He eventually felt comfortable going to a place he couldn't stand, trusting that the waves, his mother, and his growing abilities would bring him to the shore.

As I watched him get more confident, I made subtle spiritual observations. We talked about his understanding of God while waist-deep in the water. I told him Jesus walked on the water (we can take risks!), and our sins are thrown into the sea of forget-fulness (we don't need to live in the past!). We talked about how water once covered the whole earth (God is powerful!) and a man named Jonah lived three days under the sea (God calls us to follow him). We talked about how Jesus used water to baptize (we can identify with him!) and how he described himself as living water (we find refreshment in him!). There are so many ways God has used this remarkable element to teach us about himself.

I thought while out there in the waves about my own spiritual journey. Sometimes I get into the deep waters (feel over-whelmed, or lonely or afraid) and wonder, *Am I alone? Does Jesus see me?* When I have those questions, I have to remind myself of what is true and let my head guide my heart. That way, regardless of how I am feeling, the truth I can stand on is this: I am never alone. God is always with me.

When I put my kids to bed, I share with them these verses. When I am feeling scared of anything—a car coming too fast, a doctor's appointment, a conversation, an upcoming test, whatever—I read Psalm 121:

> I lift up my eyes to the mountains—
>> where does my help come from?
> My help comes from the LORD,
>> the Maker of heaven and earth.
> He will not let your foot slip—
>> he who watches over you will not slumber;
> indeed, he who watches over Israel
>> will neither slumber nor sleep.
> The LORD watches over you—
>> the LORD is your shade at your right hand;
> the sun will not harm you by day,
>> nor the moon by night.
> The LORD will keep you from all harm—
>> he will watch over your life;
> the LORD will watch over your coming and going
>> both now and forevermore.

I am learning to trust the Lord as my Captain (even when I am in waters over my head), as my Lifeguard (when I feel those waves relentlessly coming), and as my Guide (when I've lost the way home). He is there for me and is there for you, in all circumstances, all the time. No matter what happens, he will never leave.

Is that hard to believe? The people you will read about in the coming pages have at one time or another felt like they were alone. As they voiced their questions to God—*Do you see me? Do you care? Have you left me too?*—God did for them what he does best.

He reached out.

He came for them.

He listened.

He acted.

He healed.

Now they know—they were never alone. He was working on their behalf even before they realized it.

I am going to introduce you to some pretty spectacular young men and women in the coming chapters. You are going to meet Daniela, a Mexican girl I have known since she was young. Dani suffered a medical tragedy and waited and watched as God listened to her cries—the ones she said out loud and the ones she only whispered. He came for her in some surprising ways.

You'll also hear the story of Gervens, a Haitian boy who is blind, and who stole my heart the first time I met him years ago. His surprising gift of music has lifted his spirit and given him a vision for his future. When I read his story, I marvel that what is important to us is important to God. He is the God of details.

It will be a joy to introduce you to my Nigerian friend Happy and the American middle schoolers who made her life their priority. It's inspiring to hear how far she's come, and it's inspiring to see what happens when people lay down their lives for others.

One of the most dramatic stories you'll read is Tanya's. I remember everything about where I was when I first met her and heard her story. I couldn't wait to put it on paper and share it with you. It's an unbelievable testimony of God's attention to detail and his plan for our lives.

Finally, you'll meet Mario. I couldn't be prouder of him, working his way through college and growing through and from the tragedy surrounding his life. He took an enormous risk, and in reading his story, you'll be encouraged to do the same.

Regardless of who you are reading about and what they stir in you, I pray you'll be confident of this: God never leaves us alone. He is with you wherever you go.

Chapter 1

DANIELA'S WISH

MEXICO

Monterrey

Mexico City

Daniela knew something was wrong. Her sisters were crying, and her mom was crying, but she didn't know why.

"Qué pasó?" she asked her sister. Daniela pointed ahead to a field. There was an open playground built on the side of a hill, with colorful bars to climb and swing on. There were lots of kids crawling all over it, but not in uniforms, so Daniela knew right away it wasn't a school. *Must be a park*, she thought to herself.

Her older sister shook her head and closed her eyes, as if she didn't want to see it. If four-year-old Daniela could have understood the conversation between her mom and the orphanage director, she would have heard a sad story about a bad marriage and a husband who drank too much. Her mother concluded her plea with, "*Y luego* we divorced, and as you can see, I have no options—zero options. They have to stay here."

The director nodded her head. She'd heard different versions of this story for the past ten years—ever since she first came to serve at this children's home in Monterrey, Mexico. The stories came from different voices, and were about different families, but they always had the same ending. She began her typical speech, explaining their policies and the mother's rights: "You can see them on the weekends, and check them out for the holidays . . ."

In the weary mother's mind, the director's voice droned on and on. The words all seemed to run

POST CARD

CORRESPONDENCE

Qué pasó? means "What happened?"
Y luego means "And then."
Spanish is Mexico's most commonly spoken language. However, the Mexican government recognizes 68 indigenous languages as official national languages as well.

together. She nodded automatically, like a robot, as the director explained about where her children would sleep and eat and play from now on. But her eyes stared past the director's face, past the walls of this place, to the three little faces of her daughters. She saw the fear and sadness in the eyes of the two older girls. It was not an unfamiliar sight. Difficult and frightening scenes with the girls' father flashed through her brain—times he had been drunk and angry.

But then her eyes came to rest on little Daniela, spinning around and hopping up and down, totally unaware of the immense change about to come to her life. And she heard Daniela's sweet voice asking her sisters when they could go out and play with the other kids. The mother swallowed the pain that was twisting up inside her and signed the papers the director asked her to sign, holding on to the desperate hope that she was doing the right thing. That this would be better for her children. *Here they will be safe and healthy,* she thought. *They will have a chance to be happy . . . someday.*

Before she knew what had happened, her feet were taking her out of the home, through the gate, and down the road. She forced herself not to look back.

Daniela's sisters later told her about most of the rest of that day—Daniela had little memory of it herself, just floating pieces that sometimes seemed to fit together . . . and sometimes didn't.

Their mom didn't take advantage of her visitation privileges or the home-for-the-holiday option. It was too hard for her to see the girls, to answer their questions, and to listen to them cry each time she left. Weighted down with pain and guilt, she let the weekend visiting times pass by. Then summer too moved on. She came when she could—but the girls felt she was never really *there*. As each year passed by, she became more and more distant.

Daniela's mother didn't mean to hurt her

children. Rather, her thinking was that if she pulled back, and they loved her less, it would hurt them less. So she devised a strategy that included not only infrequent visits but also, when she did see her daughters, she wouldn't hug them or look them in the eyes.

After years of this treatment, it started to work. The girls didn't run to the office when told their mother was there. In fact, sometimes they purposely stalled to punish her. They learned how to manipulate their mom—capitalizing on her guilt, asking for things they didn't need just to see her bring them. When visits did occur, they weren't healthy, and neither side felt loving or loved.

It didn't take the girls long to get used to the routines and responsibilities of their new home. They made new friends and went to school, and played and ate and slept. In some ways, Daniela's life looked very much like that of any other little girl, and in some ways, nothing like it at all.

Daniela relied almost solely on her sisters for nurturing. They did their best to mother her, comforting her when she was sad or helping her learn little things like how to get dressed by herself, brush her hair, and make her bed. But they were just children too, and couldn't see all that Daniela needed. She had a series of caregivers in these years, and each one did their best to provide for the needs of Daniela and the many other children under their care.

The time came for Daniela's graduation from elementary school, and the children's home invited Daniela's mother to the ceremony for students and their families. To everyone's surprise, she came!

"Felicidades, hija." She shyly handed Daniela a balloon she had purchased on the way. It was shiny, with the English word "Congratulations!" on it. She had worried over what to bring as a gift. In the store she had considered choosing flowers or candy, but in the end she thought the balloon would leave the longest impression on her daughter. It cost much more

than her bus fare, but it was beautiful and colorful and bright. As she held tight onto the string wrapped around her hand, she hoped it was worth it.

"*Mira,* Gaby! Look!" Daniela took the balloon and ran off to show her friends. Her friends took pictures with their cameras while her mother looked on from a distance. It seemed like Daniela liked the balloon, but her mother never knew for sure. The girl never circled back around to say thank you, or to talk to her at all. She just waved to her mother later as the woman walked off the school campus and headed for the bus stop. It was time for Daniela's mother to get back for the afternoon shift she had in the factory. If she was late again, she would be fired.

POST CARD

PONDENCE

Felicidades, hija means "Congratulations, daughter."

Mira means "look."

She doesn't care that I was here. She doesn't care that I'm her mother. She is better off without me. These thoughts kept running through her mind as she made her way through the crowd. "I won't be coming back," she said to the staff at the children's home on her way out. Her voice filled with emotion. "Tell her good-bye." She spat the words out with a bit of regret and a bit of hostility. And then, before anyone could say anything else, the woman turned sharply and hurried away—back down the road, back to where she lived in pain for the choices she'd made and for choices that had been made for her.

Not too far away from where Daniela and her sisters lived, across the border, another little girl grew up. She played and ate and went to school, like Daniela did, but her life was very different from Daniela's.

Annita was excited as she packed her bag and prepared for her travels. She had just finished celebrating her own graduation, and now had a degree from graduate school. But she had some dreams she wanted to fulfill before real life—a job, or at least looking for one—began. One of those dreams was serving on a mission trip. She had been looking forward to visiting Mexico and volunteering in an orphanage. She didn't know what exactly to expect, but she did have an extra measure of confidence—having grown up in south Texas, so close to the Mexican border and where many Spanish-speaking families lived, she could speak Spanish well.

~~~~~~~~~~~~~~~~~~~~~~~

"We are headed over now to a children's home with approximately seventy children." Annita listened intently as the leader stood on a porch giving her group their instructions for the day. "We will be having a cookout, and I'll give everyone a job, so stay where you can hear me once we get there. You might hand out ketchup, pour drinks, flip burgers, or entertain kids in line. Just smile and feel free to try out any Spanish you know; they will laugh and help you out. Most of all, have fun! Today our goal is to leave the children with the impression that they are seen and delighted in."

That was an easy assignment, and the day flew by. Annita met so many children. They wanted to know where she was from, what she liked to do, and a hundred other things. She translated all day for the other group members.

Daniela watched as the group of strangers made their way among the children. She eagerly got in line to receive food—the food they got when visitors came always seemed to taste better somehow. But when one of the volunteers smiled at her, she looked away quickly. She felt shy. *Plus*, she thought, *it's no use making friends with them. They'll all go away soon, just like the others.* She ran off to look for her sisters.

One of the staff members of the children's home debriefed the volunteers later that night. "Some of you have been obedient in coming here," she said, "but when the week is done, even though you'll be glad you came, you'll be ready to head home. Thank you for coming. We pray this week will be something you never forget as you pray and give later on." She smiled and continued, "But some of you are gaining more energy as the week goes on, and you can't imagine leaving. God might be stirring something in you, a heart to engage more regularly with children, either here or in your hometown. Feel free to talk with us about how you are feeling. We'd love to hear from you!"

Annita knew right away which group she was in. She already felt like it would be hard to leave at the end of the week. One of the staff approached her that day and asked if she would consider staying and working as a caregiver for the older girls' dorm. She wasn't sure. It was a big decision, and there were so many emotions and thoughts running through her mind.

Is this what you have for me, Lord?

Daniela pulled the covers up to her chin and lay staring at the ceiling. She thought about all the events of the day, and she could see the faces of some of the visitors in her mind. They were always smiling—these people who came to help at the children's home. They always seemed like they had something to be happy about. Daniela thought about all the different cities they must come from. She thought about riding on an airplane or a train, about traveling to faraway places—maybe even over the ocean! She tried to imagine what it would be like—bringing up pictures in her head she had seen in books or magazines or on TV. But it was hard. All she could really see were some smudges on the ceiling and a spider in the corner. She let her breath out in a long sigh and closed her eyes. *If I could really talk to them, if we could do more than color alongside one another, what would they say to me? What do they think about where we live?*

The next morning Annita woke up to other staff members chiming in, encouraging her to make a short-term commitment. "Why don't you try it out? Come for a few months and see what it would be like to live with the girls." She tried to imagine herself there, tried to remember all their names and envision putting them to bed and getting them ready for school. What could she say to them? How could God use her? By the end of the week, she had agreed to two months.

It was a challenging two months.

As the girls tested her, and as she adjusted to new living conditions and being away from her family, she kept telling herself, *You can do anything for two months.* She continually asked God to open her eyes and heart to his plan for her.

Two months became six, and soon, life in the children's home was normal for Annita. She loved all the girls she was responsible for, especially Daniela—or Dani, as she called her—one of the younger ones. It had been a challenge to convince Dani to trust her, and even more so to win over Daniela's older sisters. Annita spent many nights before bedtime having conversations like this one . . .

Annita and friends.

"You know, Dani, when God made you, he planned for every single part of you. It says in the Bible you were 'wonderfully made.'"

"What does that mean?" Daniela stole glimpses of herself in the mirror while Annita brushed her hair. She didn't really think there was anything all that wonderful about the face that looked back at her.

Annita gently pulled the girl's chin toward the reflection. "It means, look at yourself. God made all of you. He made your eyes and your hands. He made you kind and generous. He's planned a big story for you, Dani. I'm sure of it."

"Then how come you are the only one who sees that? It doesn't seem like God even notices me, let alone has plans for me." She absently slid a silky ribbon through her fingers. "I'm not sure how I feel about this story you're talking about."

"I understand that. But you know, I'm not the only one who sees you as beautiful inside and out; I'm just blessed to be the one who tells you every day."

Daniela yawned, feeling sleepy. "*Buenas noches, Annita.*"

"*Buenas noches, Hermosa.*"

The early school-day mornings were no one's

favorite. Annita grew tired of waking up at 5:30 a.m. every day too, but the girls in her dorm room depended on her.

"*Buenas días*. Time to get up," Annita announced.

She already knew which of the girls would struggle to wake up and called out their names a few times in particular. Some girls sat up on their beds, others went directly to the bathroom. Dani stayed asleep a little longer. Annita tried stroking her hair, but Dani pulled the covers over her head.

"OK," Annita announced, "when I get back with breakfast, everyone who is still in bed now needs to be up and dressed."

POST CARD

Buenas noches, Hermosa means "Good night, Beautiful."

Buenos días means "Good morning."

Annita came back just in time to see Dani sprawled on the floor, laughing!

"That's what happens when you get out of bed too quickly," she quipped. Dani slowly brought herself to her feet. "The floor must be slippery here or something. I just fell!"

But an hour later, as she headed out for school, Dani lost her balance again, falling hard on the pavement outside her dorm. This time she didn't laugh. Something was wrong.

"Annita!" she cried out. Annita came running up to her and could see panic spreading over Dani's face. "I can't walk! My legs—they feel numb. I can't control them!"

From Beth's Journal

Psalm 139 teaches us that the days of our lives are all prepared, before we've even lived one day. When circumstances feel out of our control, when what we wanted or thought isn't happening, we can be confident God is with us. Sometimes I have to remind myself that God isn't surprised or caught off guard the way I can be. He is always looking at the whole story at one time.

Dani had often felt she wasn't in control of much of her life. She couldn't control that she was in a children's home, or how often her mom visited, or even who took care of her. But she'd always been able to make choices about what she wore and, at least to some extent, where she went on campus. And certainly, she was in control of her own body. Until now.

From that point on, things progressed quickly. Soon Annita was watching as Dani was rolled away in a hospital bed, staring back into her eyes, searching Annita's face for comfort.

Annita tried to keep calm, but the day felt surreal and comforting words were difficult to find. *What was going on? Dani was healthy yesterday—what had happened to her?* She felt helpless. But she knew she had to try to help her. She made some arrangements with the other staff at the children's home, gathered some of her things, and then went to the hospital.

For the next several nights, Dani spent most of the time yelling in pain. Annita stayed with her, moving Dani's body from side to side, trying to make her comfortable. Dani could stay in the same position for only about fifteen minutes before the pain would come back. The paralysis that had affected her legs was spreading over her whole body. It was as if all her muscles were freezing up. Eventually, Dani was able to move only the right side of her face. Everything else was completely out of her control.

Her smile was now crooked, one eye was frozen shut, and her pain just kept getting worse. Doctors came and talked with Annita about an illness called Guillain-Barré syndrome, a rare disorder in which the immune system attacks the body's nerves. Normally the body's immune system is there to protect it, but for unknown reasons, in some people this illness starts to break down the communication signals between the brain and the rest of the body. So gradually, bit by bit, the muscles stop responding to the brain's commands. Along with this, the nerves can send the wrong signals to the brain, resulting in the feeling of pain. This is what was happening to Dani's body.

Dani could hear the voices of the doctors, but she was too tired and confused to understand everything they were saying. She just knew she wanted relief. "Help me . . . please, Annita, help me," she moaned. Annita came and touched her hand and stood where Dani could see her face with her one functioning eye.

"I'm right here," Annita said. Then she closed her eyes and lifted up one of many hundreds of short, silent prayers she had prayed in the past week. "God, please help us!"

Early mornings were the easiest times for Dani, when she was able to get a little rest. Annita took advantage of these times to return to the children's home for short visits and to get some rest herself.

One of these mornings, Annita was so tired and disheartened, she knew she needed to get someone to help. The nurses at the hospital were busy and could not be with Dani all the time. They could not give Dani all the attention she needed to stay comfortable. And from what the doctors had said, Dani could be in the hospital for many more days—even weeks. So Annita reached out to someone she thought might be able to help—Daniela's mother.

As she called the number she found in the files, a worrying thought passed through her mind. *Am I doing the right thing? Will Dani be angry?* But then she realized that her mother needed to be informed of her daughter's medical condition—Dani was seriously ill, and if anything went wrong, her mother would want to be there. Annita felt sure of that.

"*Hola*, Flor? This is Annita, from the children's home. I need to talk to you about Dani . . ."

"I don't want you to leave," Dani confided to Annita. "I don't like it when you're gone. Please hurry back. I don't want to be with *her* alone."

Annita just smiled down at Dani and squeezed her motionless hand. "Don't worry. I'll be back soon." As she turned to leave the hospital room, she caught

Flor's eyes and tried to smile reassuringly, but she wasn't sure Flor got her message.

Dani rejected her mother from the moment she came to the hospital. She had lived in the children's home for ten years. In that ten years, her mother had rarely made a visit, and when she did, she always seemed cold and distant to Dani. Her mom hadn't been part of her life for a long time.

She doesn't belong here, Dani thought. *She doesn't belong to me*. Daniela hated the idea of depending on her mother for anything—and yet

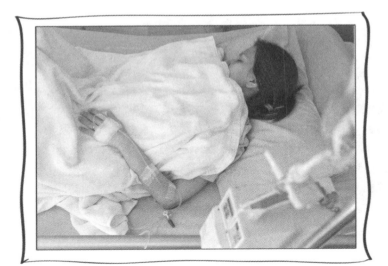

now here she was, completely stuck.

Flor wanted to help, but caring for her daughter was not easy—and Dani didn't make it any easier for her. The girl could not hide her feelings. Flor knew her daughter wanted her to leave. Every time Annita left them together, they both spent much of that time just waiting anxiously for Annita to return.

One night, Annita was walking back to the hospital, trying to hurry because she knew Dani and Flor would be waiting for her to come. She felt something stirring in her heart—it felt like hope. She prayed, *God do the impossible. You are the one who makes all things possible. Heal her. Heal Dani.*

Later that evening, as she gently moved Dani's legs to exercise her muscles, she asked Dani, "Do you want me to sing you to sleep like I always do at home?"

Dani nodded, closing her eyes.

Annita sang softly, and except for the usual beeps and whirring sounds of the hospital monitors, the room was quiet. After a while, she thought Dani had dropped off to sleep. But then she heard a small voice ask, "How many days until Christmas?"

Annita stopped singing. "It's soon, but remember, Christmas will happen wherever we are."

"Do you think I will still be here? Will you be with me? Will my mom be here?" Most of Dani's face was still frozen, but she focused her good eye straight up at Annita.

Things had started to become a little easier between Dani and her mother—they were learning how to live together again, how to talk to each other, and how to lean on each other. Dani was realizing

how much
she needed
Flor—
how it
felt good
after all these years for her
mom to be taking care of her.

Flor was becoming more relaxed around her daughter as well, but she still worried about her. Like Dani, she had lots of questions in her heart about what was going to happen. *Will she get better? What happens if she can't ever walk again?*

All these thoughts passed through Annita's mind as she quickly grasped for a good way to respond to Dani's questions. "I don't know where you'll be. But I do have a question for *you*. What do you want this year?"

She didn't even have to think about it. "That's easy," Dani said. "To be all better. And out of here. I think I want to be with my mom and my sisters."

Dani's lip started shaking—her emotions coming out. "I even want to go to church at the children's home— and you know how I never want to go. When I get better, I'm *always* going to go to church, and I'll be in the front—dancing."

"Why don't we pray for that?" Annita asked. "Let's pray God will help you get released from the hospital for Christmas, so you can celebrate with your family."

The words were already out before Annita realized what she had just said. Her faith spoke before her mind could stop her.

As Annita prayed out loud for Daniela, her own silent prayer went up to God: *Oh, Jesus, it's possible, isn't it? I know you can do all things. Can you give her this wish for Christmas?*

Over the next several days, Annita noticed small changes in the way Dani and her mom treated each other. After ten years of being apart, they were start- ing to act like mother and daughter again.

Flor was doing little things for Dani, like brushing her hair. And Dani, who still could move only one side of her face, smiled her crooked smile up at her mom. Now when she had to leave, Flor would hug her daughter good-bye, instead of just barely whispering a hurried *adiós* as she left.

Then one day Annita saw Flor kiss her daughter, her baby girl, tenderly on the cheek. Dani smiled again.

Annita realized she was watching a different kind of miracle—one no one had even prayed for! God had heard what Flor and Dani needed, and he had answered. He had given them each other.

Jesus, you've done it again, Annita thought. *You showed up where no one thought you would be. Thousands of years ago it was in a manger—but today you're here in this Mexican hospital, in the heart of a once-abandoned child.*

On December 20, 2013, Dani was released from the hospital. Even though the cold air stiffened her muscles, Dani broke into a sideways grin. Annita's last view of that hospital was Flor pushing her daughter's wheelchair through the glass doors.

After spending so much time with her mother caring for her in the hospital, Dani knew something special had happened. Flor could sense it too, but they recognized there was a lot more growing and changing and learning ahead—for both of them. At the children's home, Dani would continue her regime of medicine and physical therapy, with a personal nurse to monitor her care. Annita was ready to help Dani as well, and was glad to have her back at the home.

That Christmas, Dani spent the day with her mother and sisters. It was a beautiful day, but there was still a lot of healing to be done, both in Dani's body and in her heart.

As Flor got ready to leave after her visit, Dani awkwardly hugged her mother good-bye. "*Gracias, Mamá*," she said quietly. Her muscles were still largely unresponsive, although she could feel tiny changes. Something was happening, but it was hard to not be discouraged about coming back from the hospital in a body she didn't recognize.

"*Gracias, hija.*" Flor squeezed her daughter tightly for a second and walked out the same gate she

POST CARD

CORRESPONDENCE

Gracias, Mamá means "Thank you, Mama."

Gracias, hija means "Thank you, daughter."

had gone through more than a decade ago, when she had left Daniela and her sisters at the home.

But this time was different. Flor did not feel desperate or discouraged. This time, she had hope.

For the next several months, Dani continued to endure intense physical therapy. It was a real struggle, even with her friends and sisters all helping her. She couldn't yet go to school, so she felt lonely and bored most of the time. Then, when the girls *were* around, she'd hear stories about things her friends were doing, and frustration would spring up inside her. *Why can't I do those things too? Why am I stuck in this body?*

Dani doing physical therapy.

It was hard for Dani to come up with the will to challenge herself every day. But in this period of her recovery, many people rallied around her. Annita faithfully coordinated her care—which included 24-hour nursing care, other caregivers who encouraged her, and Dani's mother too. All of them took shifts to help with the exercises that had to be done every day so Dani's arms and legs could become stronger. And they all offered encouraging words, or sometimes a funny story, or a Scripture, or a prayer, or even just a bit of entertaining local news—anything to keep her spirits up.

The church on the campus where Daniela lived was up a huge, steep hill, and climbing the many stairs up to it was a ritual she had performed every Wednesday and Sunday for most of her childhood. When she finally felt up to going to church, there were many obstacles—including physical limitations.

"I know it'll be hard up the hill, Annita. But I want to go and be with everyone," Daniela insisted.

"Relax," Annita sighed. "I didn't say you couldn't go. I'm just not sure how we'll make it happen. Hold on." Dani watched as Annita went outside. *What is she doing?*

Soon enough, Dani understood Annita's plan. A whole group of people came filing into her room and surrounded her wheelchair. "If it's church you want to go to, we can't let a little thing like rocks and a hill stop you," said one of the men who served in the home.

With their help, Dani rolled out of the dorm and into the sun. The friends laughed and joked as they pushed and pulled Dani in her wheelchair up the hill, all the way to the entrance of the church. It was a true picture of how many people had gathered to love her through this time.

Daniela continued to have good days and bad ones; she grew up more in the following months than she had in the last few years. She continued with her physical therapy every day, and the children's home found a tutor who brought school to her. Her mom's visits came more regularly, and Daniela saw something she hadn't ever seen in her before—commitment.

One day as they were having a meal together, Flor blurted out, "What do you think about coming home with me someday?" Dani's mama had been practicing this conversation for weeks, and now in the moment, she was afraid and wished she could swallow the words up.

Daniela stopped the spoon that was halfway to her mouth. She didn't say anything and just sat there frozen for a moment. Then she continued to eat, now in an awkward silence.

"Never mind, maybe it's not a good idea. You wouldn't have your own room, and I'm sure you would want that." Flor's voice trailed off, and she looked intently out the window at something that suddenly seemed very interesting.

Daniela smiled. She hadn't imagined it would ever be an option to move in with her mother. She wasn't sure right now how she felt about it, but it was nice to even be able to consider it.

The spring wore into summer, and Daniela kept getting stronger. There was no big magical moment when she jumped out of her wheelchair, but little by little, she had been gaining back the control of her muscles. First in her face, then her arms and upper body. By the time summer came, Dani was able to stand and even walk short distances on her own.

And as Dani's body was healing, little by little her relationship with her mom was growing too. Dani didn't even know it, but Flor had been working hard all the time, trying to save money and create a life in which she could offer something to her daughters.

One Sunday afternoon, Flor came to visit. She looked confident as she declared proudly, "I've been working hard for our future. I found a new house, where you can have your own room. I want you to come home."

Dani couldn't believe it. For years her mom had kept her distance, not touching her, not even showing up to visit. But now this strong woman stood in front of her, reaching out to Dani, promising to be with her.

At first, Dani didn't know what to think. She gave her mother a shy hug and told her she'd need some time to think it through.

Can I trust her? she wondered.

The topic of Dani returning home became a regular part of conversation when Annita was with Dani. There was a lot to consider, especially since she was still recovering from her illness and would continue to need help with her exercises and medical care for some time to come. Annita loved Dani greatly, but she knew this was a decision the girl needed to make on her own. She led her through laying out the pros and cons of being with her mother. She helped her consider the potential risks Dani wasn't even aware of.

But they also talked about trust—about who we trust ourselves to, and why it matters. Annita explained how she herself had to trust in God's plan for her when she first came to the children's home. She talked about how she worked through that decision and how important it was to listen to voices who cared about her and knew God's truth. And she shared how sometimes you have to just believe God has a plan, even when you don't know what it is or don't like how things look right now. God always has a plan, and he's always with us every step of the way.

One sunny summer day, Dani was walking with Annita's help when she announced, "This week, I want to walk to church." Annita's eyebrows shot up in surprise, but she didn't say a word. Dani continued, "I asked God to make me well. I told God I wanted to go home and live with my mother. I told him I would trust him. And now I want to dance in his church, just like I promised I would."

Annita just nodded and smiled; words were no longer necessary between them. That Sunday, she and Dani left extra time to climb the stairs together. It was a hot July morning, and sweat poured down Daniela's face with the effort to make it up those steps and inside the church. But she smiled the biggest smile as she moved to the music all the way to the front row.

Have you ever been in a situation where you had no idea what was going to happen next? What was that like?

Have you ever felt like no one could understand what you were going through? Dani must have certainly felt that way at times. But God knew. Psalm 34:18 tells us that "The Lord is close to the brokenhearted and saves those who are crushed in spirit." Tell about a time when you either felt that God was close to you, or a time when you really wanted him to be with you.

Chapter 2

GERVENS'S VISION

The sun slowly peeked above the horizon, casting light over the mountains and onto the plains of Haiti, as the Caribbean Sea kissed the island's shores. Another day of life had begun. As the sun rose higher into the sky, the streets filled with people. A woman lit a handful of charcoal, preparing her pot of rice and beans to sell at noon. Another woman arranged the soaps, lotions, and other goods in her basket, hoping to make a small profit to feed her children that day. Men on motos (motorcycle taxis) gathered on the corners of the streets, waiting for a phone call from a regular customer or someone just passing by who needed a ride somewhere. Other men carried boxes full of bottled drinks, each sold for about thirty *gourdes*. Still others, clad in business attire and carrying briefcases, boarded public transportation to make their way to an office in downtown Port-au-Prince.

Children dressed in uniforms walked to school, the smaller ones led by the hand of a parent or care-giver, while the older kids could be seen hanging out with groups of their peers.

The heat from the faithful sun grew more intense as the morning progressed, and the air felt heavy, full of the smell of burning trash and frying food. This was life for most of the Haitian people, trying to survive another day, trying to make a small wage to keep their family afloat, trying to make their way in a world that seems to have forgotten them.

This story began sixteen years ago, in Cabaret, a

POST CARD

CORRESPONDENCE

Gourdes are the units of currency in Haiti. One gourde is about two cents in the US. The term is thought to have come from Haiti's French background, from a French word that means "sack," or "purse"—as in, a purse for holding money. Haitians speak Haitian Creole as their national language, although French is also considered an official language of the country.

town about twenty miles north of Haiti's capital, Port-au-Prince. There was a man there named Stephen, who was a music teacher. One afternoon, this music teacher crossed paths with a student returning home from school. The young woman walked by him, and as soon as she caught his eye, he was captivated. He approached her and asked her name.

"Kimberly."

The two became friends, and eventually they fell in love. The wedding took place—their new life together began.

Years passed and the couple became a family of five. They had two babies: a girl and a boy. But they also adopted a young boy, the son of their friend, who was not able to support or care for her child. Life was busy, and Stephen juggled a few different jobs so his family was able to eat. He was not only a music teacher but also now a carpenter and a moto driver. He did all he could so at the end of the day, he could go to bed knowing that his family was happy.

Valentine's Day, February 14, 2003, was another sweltering day in Haiti. The sun beat down upon the dry and dusty plain of Port-au-Prince as Stephen waited in the hospital. Kimberly was giving birth to their fourth and last child. They named their baby boy Gervens Ulysses (pronounced JOE-venz you-LISS-eez).

The first year of his life flew by, but when Gervens began to walk, they noticed something wasn't quite right. As he took small steps, he ran into things—big things. He ran into their bed, their dining room table, the chair in the corner—he was not avoiding these objects like most babies would. They assumed he was just learning, but weeks later, there was no change. Stephen and Kimberly took their son to a doctor.

That was when their lives changed.

"Gervens is blind," the doctor told them. "He's been blind since birth." The doctor explained that if the boy had been operated on immediately when he was born, the problem could have been fixed. But unfortunately, because of the lack of good health care, there was no one to attend to Gervens's eyes. "He will grow up blind," the doctor announced. "He will have to learn how to get around in a world he cannot see."

The couple returned home with their son, devastated by the news. In their culture, those with disabilities were seen as outcasts—worthless. People assumed that they couldn't contribute anything useful to others. There were very few jobs available for anyone—it was almost impossible for a person with a disability to find work.

That night, Stephen and Kimberly lay down on their mat—each silently wondering what kind of future their son could have. *What exactly are we supposed to do with him?*

Kimberly spoke first. "How will he go to school? How will he learn?"

Stephen echoed back, "How will he ever work? How can I protect him?"

The longer they thought about these questions, the more discouraged they became. Hours later,

It is estimated that 800,000 to 1,000,000 people in Haiti live with disabilities—thousands became amputees after the earthquake of 2010. The good news is that as Haiti is undergoing reconstruction, leaders are striving to make new buildings more accessible to all Haitians.

Kimberly was still tossing and turning. "Are you asleep?" she whispered to her husband.

"I can't escape my thoughts." He punched the ground and mourned quietly for his son's life and the experiences Gervens would never have.

It wasn't long before light seeped through the tattered cloth they used as a window covering. Even the sun seemed weary as Stephen lifted himself out of his bed and put his feet heavily on the dirt floor. Today he would be fitting a door for a home in his town. He was glad for the work, though he wished

POST CARD

CORRESPONDENCE

Orevwa means "good-bye."

he could stay in bed a little longer. He buttoned the shirt his wife had washed by hand just the day before, and tightened his belt around his waist. He grabbed the work bag with his few belongings inside, and his gaze fell on Gervens, whose eyes were just beginning to open. Stephen's heart sank. *My son can see nothing*. Not his mother, not his brothers and sister, not the bed he slept on or the dusty sunbeams streaming into the small house. Caught up in emotion, Stephen mumbled, "*Orevwa,*" and stepped out the front door.

The missionary smiled. No matter how many times he watched it happen, it always brought him joy to see children of all ages as they ran to join in with the group. He and other ministry leaders had been hosting these kids' clubs for some time, but had recently branched out to reach a new village. Playing games, singing songs, listening to Bible stories—the young hearts soaked up all the attention like parched plants in a rainstorm. All the kids were eager for something to do—something to take their minds off the ever-present worries of home. Most came from families who were living on little or no income. Some were sick. Almost all of them were hungry.

I can't feed them all, but at least I can give them some hope. He prayed, asking God to give him the words that would bring peace and truth and love to these beautiful faces. As the music started up, the kids broke out in a familiar dance, worshipping God from head to toe. The man opened his eyes to look around. A thought came to him and he prayed one more time. *And Father, be with the ones who didn't make it here today.*

By the time Gervens was six years old, his family had moved to a town farther away from the city. It was a small village in a more rural, more poor area. For a while after they moved there, he had tried to play outside with the other kids and make new friends. But he soon learned that they didn't want to be friends with him. Instead, they made fun of him. In some ways, he didn't understand it. He felt the same as he always had—and he could play games too. But he knew he was different from the other kids—even his siblings sometimes acted like they didn't want him around. He couldn't see their frustrated faces, but he could hear their sighs and their muttered complaints.

He began to feel like a burden to everyone, including his parents. He tried to help, but no one in the family let him do much. They said he was in the way. His mother often didn't even let him out of the house. She knew she couldn't keep him safe out there, and she worried what the other kids would do to him. So she made him stay inside as much as she could.

Gervens tried to do what his mother asked, but it was hard. He got so bored sitting in the house by himself, with nothing to do. What made it worse was that he could hear all the voices of kids outside, having fun together. He heard them one afternoon— he could tell from the sounds of their feet that they were running together in the same direction. A missionary from another town had been visiting their village lately, and Gervens knew everyone liked going to the kids' club this man and his friends set up for them. He had heard his siblings talking about it. Gervens had tried many times to go along with all the other kids, but every time he ventured out of his house to join in on the fun, he got pushed back. *Maybe today will be different.*

He quickly put on his clothes—a faded yellow T-shirt and a pair of shorts. He slipped on his sandals, which were practically falling apart, and bounced out the door, eager to find out what he had been missing all this time. His mother turned around from her work in the kitchen in time to see her son's head zipping past the window. She quickly wiped her hands and raced out after him, but she was too late. Gervens had moved fast to catch up with the other kids, almost jogging. Despite not being able to see, his hearing helped him know exactly where to go, and soon he had disappeared among a crowd of other excited children.

His mother stopped and caught her breath. She feared the rejection that she knew would come to her child, but she also knew she couldn't stop it from happening. Not this time. She turned around to go home and wait for him, hoping his siblings would find him and bring him back. *Please come home safe.*

Gervens couldn't wait to get there. He heard children laughing and teasing one another and singing—it all sounded like so much fun. As he got swept up in the crowd, Gervens reached out his arms instinctively to feel around and get his bearings. He groped for a place to sit down, but bumped into a pole and fell into someone's lap. An older boy's voice turned from excitement to anger as Gervens felt a hard fist hit his side. He tried to get up and out of the way, but two hands pushed down with force onto his back, sending him off balance again. Gervens toppled to the ground onto his side.

Harsh laughter rang in his ears. Gervens curled up and covered his head with his arms, trying to drown out the noise. But it just wouldn't stop. The kids kept laughing at him.

Why did I come? I don't belong here. I don't even know where "here" is. He could feel the sting of the tears underneath his eyelids, but he kept his eyes shut tight.

A hand rested softly on his shoulder. Gervens stiffened up, fearing another kid was going to hit him. But instead, a gentle voice said, "Come with me." Another hand, large and strong, grabbed his, and he felt himself being easily lifted from the dirt. "What's your name?" the mysterious voice asked. Gervens slowly mumbled an answer.

"A little louder," the voice calmly prompted.

The boy mustered the strength to get his name out again without crying. "My name is Gervens."

"Gervens? That's a great name." The voice was peaceful and encouraging. Gervens squeezed the stranger's hand tightly as the man led him through the crowd. Gervens could hear him asking the other kids if they knew where he was from.

"Excuse me!" a girl's voice called out. "Follow me. I'll take you to his house."

The girl led Gervens and his new friend to his home. The missionary, who had also left the gathering to find out who this little boy was, followed along behind them. They all arrived at the boy's simple *kay*, only to find Gervens's mother waiting at the door. Still a beautiful woman, her face showed the wear of living a difficult life, like most Haitians. She welcomed them to join her on the porch as she pulled out the few chairs she had inside her home.

POST CARD

Kay means "home" or "house."

"Is he OK?" she began. "Did it happen again?" She struggled with finding the right words.

The Haitian who led Gervens home had many questions. "How old is he? Is he in school?"

They talked, and the missionary leaned in to learn more of Gervens's story. The woman shared openly and brokenly how the other kids in the village had made fun of him. She confessed that she kept him inside as much as possible in order to protect him.

"I didn't know he had snuck out, until it was too late."

The missionary listened intently, wondering how he could help. Then he asked, "Could I take Gervens to the eye doctor to see if there is anything else that can be done for him?"

POST CARD

CORRESPONDENCE

Wi means "yes."

In many Haitian words, the French influence can easily be heard. The Haitian wi sounds just like the French word oui (pronounced like WEE)—both mean "yes."

Kimberly hung her head, both in defeat and shame. She was tired. She wanted to be a good mother, but she didn't know what else to do for her son. *"Wi."* She answered without regret.

The missionary offered some gentle instructions. "I am not sure how long this will take. Make him up a bag with some clothes and things, so if he needs to stay a few nights with me, he'll be prepared."

Kimberly retreated inside and packed a small backpack with the things Gervens would need: clothes, underwear, and his toothbrush. She handed the pack to the missionary and placed Gervens's hand in his.

Reaching down to her son, she whispered, "Behave. I will see you soon."

As she watched them walk off together, she felt hopeful for the future of her son for the first time.

That afternoon, Stephen returned home from work to find his wife sitting on their bed. He noticed Gervens was not in the room and became concerned right away. "Where is he? Do I need to go out and look for him again?"

"No, you won't believe what happened!" she answered. "He did slip out when I wasn't looking, but some people brought him back. One of them was that missionary man. Gervens had been hurt by some village children, and they offered to take him to a doctor for his wounds, and for *his eyes.*"

A mixture of relief and disbelief washed over Stephen. "Really? They think they can help him?" He wondered who they were. Did they want money? Kimberly answered with what she knew. She reassured her husband that they just wanted to help. Stephen sat down beside her and put his head in his hands. "It's hard to believe it . . . I think this is the first time anyone outside of this house has shown him any compassion." He embraced his wife, full of emotions he could not explain.

Not long after that day, on January 12, 2010, a
massive earthquake struck Haiti, killing hundreds of
thousands of people and displacing even more from
their homes. In the village where Gervens had lived,
many people suffered. The walls of Gervens's family
home cracked and the ceiling crumbled, opening up.
His family packed up what they could and picked
their way through rubble to a nearby village, along
with several of their neighbors. But Gervens wasn't
with them.

In the hours and days that followed the quake, the missionary worked quickly to gather resources to help people in desperate need. The home where he lived and took care of children—called the Lighthouse—had been built well. Although they had all felt the shaking, the walls around them stood strong.

The man stopped in to check on the kids, who had all gathered together to comfort one another. His gaze fell on Gervens, and he couldn't help but stop and thank God that the boy was there at the Lighthouse instead of with his family when the earthquake hit. It would have been terrifying for him—feeling the trembling earth and hearing the cracking walls. It's doubtful he would have even made it out alive in all the confusion that followed, with an unstable roof overhead and no sight to help him navigate his surroundings. Gervens's senses would have been overwhelmed and jumbled; he could have been trapped or lost. Instead, he was safe and well taken care of, surrounded by his new friends.

Gervens was glad to be at the Lighthouse. He did not know exactly what had happened to his house or his family, but he knew he would have been in their way after the earthquake. His first week at the home stretched into a month, and the month became a year. After a while, his own family sent word that they could not care for him full-time anymore. But the Lighthouse staff were more than willing to welcome him into their family.

At the end of that year, he had changed so much. He felt different—stronger. He was no longer that little boy who was constantly picked on in the village. Now he had friends who would protect him, and people who understood how to care for him.

Gervens (left) and his friend.

His guardians had taken him to see several different eye doctors, all of whom concluded that nothing more could be done to correct his vision. For many children this news would have been devastating, but Gervens was different. As he grew up, he developed a deeper sense of the world around him. He could see things in a way others could not.

For several years, Gervens attended school with the other kids who lived at the Lighthouse orphanage. But it was difficult and often frustrating. The school was not equipped to teach a child who couldn't see. Gervens had trouble advancing—he missed what the teacher wrote on the chalkboard and the words on his homework. The other kids tried to help him, but slowly he fell behind.

"You don't know this kid, but he's incredible . . ."
Gervens's houseparent continued on, describing the
boy's gifts and telling his story. He had come to plead for
a spot for Gervens at a special school for blind children.
The headmaster of the school nodded patiently as he
listened.

"I am sure he is wonderful; all our students are."
The man began gathering up some papers. It was clear
he felt the meeting was over. "But we have a protocol.
Put his name on the list, and when something opens up,
we'll tell you."

A year passed by. These special schools were very
hard to find in Haiti, and it was even harder for students
to get accepted into them. So Gervens's name remained
on the waiting list.

But he was never alone. God saw Gervens and was
working on his behalf all along—weaving a future for him
that no one could imagine.

One day, the call came.

"Is this the home of Gervens Ulysses?"

His houseparent's heart skipped a beat. "*Wi,*" he
answered. "Is this the school?"

"I am pleased to inform you that Gervens has
been accepted for fall enrollment . . ."

Soon the sounds of cheering and crying and dancing came from the kitchen. All the children rushed over to find out what had happened.

Gervens started crying and didn't even know

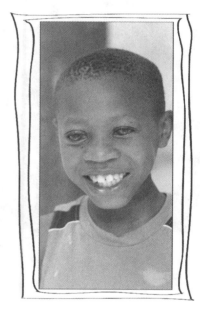

why. He just *felt* like it was a special day. Then his houseparents sat him down and explained that, for the first time in his life, he was going to have the opportunity to read and to write, and to learn with other kids who were exactly like him. Gervens couldn't believe it. He was so happy, but also a little scared. His best friend at the Lighthouse leaned over and whispered to him, "I don't want you to go to a different school without me, but maybe there, no one will make fun of you."

As Gervens waited for his new school to start, he turned his attention to his greatest love—music. Because of his blindness, Gervens had developed an incredible gift for hearing and using sound. When he moved around the house or the neighborhood, he used what he heard to know which way to go and how to avoid obstacles. He had spent the first several years of his life listening to all the instruments his music teacher dad played. And now, of all the sounds he heard every day, music was his favorite, especially the sound of the piano.

After he moved into the Lighthouse, he became used to the visitors who would come to help out at the orphanage and play with the kids. These visitors often brought little gifts. They gave Gervens toys that made noise or music of some kind—his favorite was a little keyboard.

"Come, listen to me." Gervens led his housemom to his room. He had been working all morning on a song he'd heard at church the week before.

She sat patiently as he positioned himself at the keyboard and began to play. Sounds came from the instrument slowly, but beautifully, making themselves recognizable as a song she knew.

"Bon travay! Felisitasyon!" She clapped enthusiastically, and Gervens sat, triumphant, encouraged that all his hours of practicing had paid off. He began almost immediately to tackle a new song. At first, he was embarrassed when the other kids approached with their questions and comments.

"How long have you been practicing?"

"How do you know where the keys are?"

"What's this song called?"

"Do your fingers hurt?"

POST CARD

CORRESPONDENCE

Bon travay! Felisitasyon! means "Good work! Congratulations!"

Gervens stopped, recoiling his hands away from the keyboard. Frozen, he didn't know what to do.

"You don't have to stop," one kid finally complained, breaking the silence. "I was liking it—I just had a question." The other kids murmured their agreement, and Gervens began again, hearing the words circle in his mind, *I was liking it . . .*

More visitors came and went, and whenever they asked Gervens what he would like, the boy smiled and asked for a keyboard. Not the same kind of toy keyboard he already had, but a real one, with eighty-eight black and white keys. He felt like he'd made so many new friends, and so, he became more hopeful.

Maybe, it will happen. Maybe my keyboard will come. While he waited, Gervens envisioned a future where, in his new school, he could learn to read and write and, one day, be a teacher of music. It was the first time he had considered his future in a hopeful way.

From Beth's Journal

For most Haitians, it seems as though they have been forgotten. There are currently ten million people living in Haiti. In a country that's often overlooked on the map because it's so small, it's not hard to understand why so many people feel unwanted and unloved. A woman sacrifices all she has just to keep her children alive, so they might have a better future than the one she is living. A man wonders where and how his children are—the ones he left a long time ago because he didn't feel he could adequately provide for them. Many of these stories are filled with sadness because of the extreme poverty that exists in Haiti. But not all stories go untold and not all stories end in sadness, because our God is a God who never forgets. His children never struggle alone.

However, months later, no keyboard had arrived, and Gervens grew discouraged. The small toy keyboard he had once loved to practice on no longer excited him. He couldn't play all the notes he wanted to play.

Tony didn't know exactly what to expect on this trip to Haiti. He and his wife and daughter had come to the children's home to work and help in whatever ways they could. They all loved spending time with the kids. But when Tony met Gervens, he knew at once there was something special about him.

The boy seemed taken with Tony too, and he stuck close to Tony's side during the whole visit. Even though they didn't speak the same language, Gervens seemed to feel safe with the man. Perhaps he heard the soft tone in Tony's voice when he talked with his daughter. Or maybe he was just missing the love and strength of his dad. Whatever the reason, they became fast friends.

Tony was eager to learn more about this young boy and asked his houseparents, "What does Gervens want for his life? What are his dreams?"

"That's easy," his housemom replied without hesitation. "He wants a keyboard. He wants to make music."

Gervens always felt a little sad when it came time for the visitors to leave. This time he really didn't want to say good-bye to his new friends, especially Tony.

He could tell that Tony was sad to say good-bye too. "Thank you for being my friend," the man said, using a translator.

Gervens just smiled and gave him a hug.

Tony looked out the window as the plane cleared the ground and rose into the sky. He put his earbuds in and heard the first few notes of one of his favorite songs. *I must do something to help Gervens*, he thought. He wasn't sure when or how, but he knew he had to help this boy make his dream become a reality. And he knew he'd never forget Gervens.

A week later, Gervens heard the other kids whispering something about the keyboard he had asked for. *Why are they all talking about this now? What do they know that I don't? What can they see?* Every time he came into a room or walked up to kids in conversation, it seemed like everyone stopped talking.

"What are you talking about?" Gervens asked, wishing to know their secret.

"Oh, nothing," one of the kids responded. But Gervens could hear in his voice that he wasn't telling the whole truth.

Later that afternoon, Gervens heard a car horn at the gate. The kids raced downstairs and he followed them. Everyone was talking again, but this time their voices were much louder. Gervens's heart began to beat faster as he felt the excitement in the air.

The crowd of kids flowed outside and surrounded the car that was there. Gervens felt his way around to the bumper at the back of the car, and someone opened the trunk. Gervens knew what was inside even before his fingers touched the box. Many hands lifted the large, long box out of the trunk and helped to carry it all the way up the stairs and into Gervens's bedroom. Gervens skipped alongside the crowd as they went. He beamed as his fingers ran along the edge of the box, measuring out its length. Someone helped him open the box, and others worked quickly to assemble the gift.

When everything was ready, all the kids gathered around Gervens as he took his seat on the bench. His fingers gently graced the keys of the beautiful, brand-new, full-size keyboard, and he listened intently to each different tone.

"Thank you, Tony," he whispered aloud.

The following Saturday morning (and every one since), a piano teacher arrived at the home to teach Gervens how to play. After each lesson, she reiterated how intelligent he was, and how amazed she was at his ability to play without seeing the keys.

Gervens listened closely as the pastor spoke on Sunday morning. His heart was ripe to hear the message: "God is with you. On this day, if you are tired, tell him. If you are scared, tell him. If you need to feel his presence, tell him. He'll come for you. He's prepared a place for you, not just in the world to come, but in this one. There isn't anyone who is outside of his gaze. He loves us, each one."

Among the amens and hallelujahs that chorused around him, Gervens's heart sang its own song. He nodded quietly to the truth of the message that day. God did see him; this he knew. God saw him when he was a little boy, struggling in his village. He saw his parents worrying over his care. God was with him when he was bullied by other children, and he was with him in the earthquake. There was no telling how many dangers God moved out of his path daily.

And now he knew too that God had given him a gift—the gift of music. And God had a plan for him, to go to school, to feel the love of a community—maybe one day to teach music to other children.

For all this, Gervens will praise God, with words . . . and music.

Gervens prayed for a special gift from God, and God certainly blessed him with many gifts. Name some of the gifts Gervens was given— either material blessings or spiritual ones. Name some of the gifts you have been given. After you've made your list, take some time to thank God for his gifts.

Some people might look at someone like Gervens and feel sorry for him for what he lacks. But in Psalm 34:9 we read these words: "Fear the Lord, you his holy people, for those who fear him lack nothing." How would you describe the kind of fear mentioned in this verse? Why do you think the writer says that "those who fear him lack nothing"?

Chapter 3

HAPPY'S LESSONS

It was a hot day in Nigeria when Happy Ayiki was born. Never mind that it was December 1 and the rains had already washed through the region, supposedly cooling off the parched African soil. Happy's mother, Amira, wailed her way through the day, biting on tree bark and drinking a mixture of herbs. The women in her village had made the concoction for her, especially for this day. They knew how the herbs dulled the pain of childbirth.

"You can."

"It's almost time."

"You are strong."

NIGERIA

"Let your body lead."

The women of the Kisayhip community, a Rukuba tribal village, offered their advice and encouragement to Amira. She kept her eyes mostly closed. This wasn't her first baby, and she knew that no matter how much it hurt now, she'd soon forget all about it.

One of the younger women offered up honestly, "I don't know—I'm sure you can do this, but it all seems really hard." This got her some stern looks from the others and more than one elbow. Unfazed, she continued on, "You do whatever you want. Sit, stand, scream, squeeze, cry, whatever. Just try and feel more comfortable—if that's even possible."

This brought on some laughs, and the women relaxed, sitting back to watch for the arrival of the

POST CARD

CORRESPONDENCE

Yana da wata yarinya means "It's a girl" in Hausa, a commonly spoken language in Nigeria. The official language of Nigeria, however, is English.

afternoon's long-awaited gift. Amira rolled her eyes and pressed her lips together hard, silently bearing the pain of childbirth within the supportive circle of these village sisters.

Eventually, a hearty scream rang through the air. First it was Amira's, followed by the distinct cry of a newborn baby.

"*Yana da wata yarinya*! It's a girl!" The women cheered and cooed, then sang and cried. Amira laid back, exhausted. She smiled weakly and breathed out, "Her name will be Happy."

I want more *for these students.* An Ohio youth pastor looked out over the crowded room of middle school students who had gathered for Sunday morning worship. He saw some who were engaged, curious about their faith. He saw others talking to each other and more interested in hanging back than learning. The music blaring over the loudspeakers was winding down, and he knew he was up next onstage. Sighing, he thought, *I want them to see how much God has for them. How do I do that, Lord?* How could he show them God had gifted them and written them into stories bigger than what they were currently dreaming—bigger than soccer games and sleepovers. The pastor wanted his students to go out from that place feeling challenged and engaged in something life-changing.

What, Lord? he asked, as the lights went down in the room and the kids quieted to hear the morning's talk. *What is your plan? What do I tell them? Where in this world do you want to connect their lives with others?*

Amira, her husband, Yabani, and Happy lived in the village with Happy's two older brothers and sister. There they participated fully in village life, worshipping in the nearby church on Sundays, pitching in during dry-season farming, going into town when they needed supplies. It was a life of survival—full of farming, some education, village community

The village of Kisaybip.

gatherings, an occasional health crisis, weather watching, and church participation. It was a complete life, and although it was hard some days, Amira cherished it.

Then one fateful day in 2007, everything about her cherished life changed.

"What's up with that? Did you hear him? Half of what we get for Christmas? He's lost it, right?" Scott nudged his friend Chase. "And for what? To give it to kids we'll never meet? That's messed up . . ."

Chase hardly heard his friend. He was focused on the youth pastor onstage who was still talking, offering a challenge. " . . . and so when I heard about this need, I thought of you guys. I think we can raise it—right here, among you middle school students. It will mean sacrifice. Babysitting money, lawn-mowing money, and like I said, maybe even Christmas gifts. But just imagine! You! Being a part of something on the other side of the world!" Chase tried to imagine it, and he felt his heart thump harder. He didn't even know where Nigeria was, but he wanted in. *We can do this!*

I can't do this! As she wailed into the sky, Amira felt despair and doubt settle heavily on her shoulders. She didn't know if her questions even reached God. Could he hear her? Other villagers gathered in the doorframes of their huts and looked across the dust at this woman stumbling in her grief. They knew that sound—the cries of a woman left without means.

Yabani, Amira's husband, had left that morning for work as usual, pulling out of their village with his new motorbike, a tool loaned to him by his employer for his delivery job. It was common there to travel by motorbike. The streets at times were filled with hundreds of them, weaving in and out of traffic—each driver trying to get where he wanted to go faster than everyone else. It made for chaotic conditions and dangerous intersections. In one of those intersections, Yabani paid for his hurry with his life.

Several hours after Yabani was pronounced dead on the scene, the news reached Amira. Friends stopped by all throughout the next day, paying their respects or bringing small gifts to Amira. She gathered them all up, knowing that was all she had now to sustain her small family. She felt so alone.

The mother looked at three-year-old Happy. The little girl understood something was wrong, but she didn't comprehend yet what it was, or what it meant for their lives. She did not know her daddy was not coming home.

"*Ta karamin yaro*, I wish you were old enough to later remember how life has been, because it's about to get very hard. Now this is all you'll know . . ." Amira sighed. How was she to work? What could she make or do? How could she provide for or protect her children? How could she afford schooling? Who would watch

POST CARD

CORRESPONDENCE

Ta karamin yaro means "My little child."

Happy? There were so many questions she didn't have answers for. *God, are you with me? Have you left me alone?*

"We don't have enough. We need more." Chase overheard two girls talking before church. One of the girls sounded discouraged. "I heard we haven't even made it halfway to our goal. What will they do if we don't get enough?"

By now, most of the middle school students in the church were fully invested in this one big dream—to build an educational center in the middle of a Nigerian village. They wanted to do it themselves, by sacrificing half of what they'd normally get for Christmas. The adults in this congregation had been involved in missions in Nigeria for a long time, but the youth pastor wanted to offer these kids the chance to serve too. He wanted them to get caught up in something bigger than themselves. After hearing of the need for an educational center that would benefit the lives of orphaned children, the kids had made the decision together to help. By having fund-raisers and investing their allowances and gifts in a cause greater than themselves, all of them—pastor and kids alike—were looking forward to having a Christmas no one would ever forget.

But it was already early December and the dollars weren't coming in as fast as they wanted. One of the student small groups came up with the idea of recording a Christmas album. They gathered, wrote some songs, picked a few traditional favorites, and made a CD. Then they began selling them. Chase and the others became more hopeful as they watched their total offering start to grow.

Several years passed, and the time came for Happy to leave her mother's side all day and enter school. There was a public school she could walk to with her siblings, right there in the village. But the books provided to the school by the government were all in English, the official language of Nigeria. Happy didn't speak English. Amira didn't speak English. Even Happy's teachers didn't speak very much English. And so, the books were hardly ever opened.

By the end of her first year in school, Happy knew less than five words in the language the school was supposed to operate in. And since they did not have books in the local language, their lessons were sometimes inconsistent. The school was not a success, but in villages like Happy's, no one really cared whether the children ended up learning what was in books.

Happy skipped home with her sister Hannatu from classes one afternoon. To her surprise, the hut was empty. *Where is Mama? She's always here when we come home. What's wrong? What if something's happened to her like Papa?* Happy began to shout and ran back outside.

"Mama! Where are you? Answer me!" The little girl's feet pounded on the hard ground as she ran from hut to hut. "Has anyone seen my mama?"

Several of her aunties—the women in the village—came around her. Though they were not sure where Amira was, they confidently assured Happy that nothing was wrong.

Meanwhile, on the far edge of the village and well out of earshot, Amira was deep in conversation with one of the community elders.  She had lost track of time. Her only focus was getting answers—a workable solution to what was a growing problem.

"I don't know how my children will ever survive. I know they need more than they are getting right now." She shared what she could with the man but kept her most fearful thoughts to herself. *Where can they work without English? They will be destined to a difficult life like mine, working a small piece of village land, living on the whim of the weather.* The elder listened and commiserated, but he had no hope to offer.

She left her meeting feeling defeated, and walked back to her hut. There she found a hysterical Happy

From Beth's Journal

It would be a while before Amira would see an answer to her prayers. That's how it works sometimes. God is moving on our behalf, but we think he's being silent, because we can't see it yet. Even before Amira had cried out to him, God had already captured the heart of a church, communicated a need to a youth pastor, and inspired a group of kids to sacrifice—there was a lot going on. Amira was about to see it all unfold. But she couldn't see it yet. While she waited for answers—both for her children and for herself—she sat, somewhat uneasily, in her knowledge that God is good and he is in control. When the doubts come, we can find strength in knowledge—in knowing who God has been to us and who he has promised to be.

being comforted by her aunties. Amira took her daughter in her arms, and Happy's breathing eventually resumed a normal rhythm. As the girl went off to play, Amira thought, *I wish all crises could be solved so easily*.

This mother wanted more for her children—more knowledge, more chances, more opportunities to grow, more hope. She cried out her desires to God, but again wondered if he was listening at all. Her feelings told her nothing. Her fear returned. *Has he left us alone?*

It was December 18. Chase had been watching all month as the number of their total amount kept creeping up. He had already brought in a check from his parents—approximately half the amount they had been planning on spending on him that Christmas. He felt good about slashing his Christmas list in half and being a part of what was happening. He heard stories every week about the village kids in Nigeria and their schools. He heard how this educational center could change things for them in amazing ways. He even read online at home about statistics for the country. He understood the great need.

So he came that morning ready to go all in.

Heart racing, he fingered the wad of money in his pocket. Yes or no? His mind momentarily wavered.

Yes.

Before he could back out, he approached his youth pastor. He handed him a wad of cash and swallowed hard, forgetting the words he had planned to say.

"Where'd you steal this from?" his pastor joked.

"It's the earnings from my summer lawn-mowing business." Chase found his voice and looked him in the eye. "I just kept thinking this month how it'll mean more to them than it does to me."

His youth pastor grew quiet and put his arm around Chase's shoulders. "It means a lot to *me*."

Almost two years after Amira's conversation with the village elder, some missionaries from a group called Back2Back Ministries visited the village for the first time. They had lots of questions.

They asked about water—was it clean? Where did they get it? How long did it take? Was anyone getting sick? They also asked about schooling—where was the school? What kind of training and materials did it have? Were orphans being served there? And they asked about single parents and heads of households—how did widows support themselves? Who was helping them? What were their needs? How were their kids coping?

Amira grew curious about these people with all the questions. Why did they care? They were interviewing families whose mothers were widows, determining if the children were receiving adequate nutrition and education. Amira did her best to explain how much she loved her children and how she worried about what they were learning. She knew that without

English, the children would have a hard time making their way in life. Even if they graduated,

they wouldn't have the qualifications they'd need to get good jobs.

She watched the faces of the strangers carefully as she talked. Would they be able to understand? They were not Nigerians—did they know what it meant in this country to know English? How speaking English often meant the difference between living in poverty and being able to work and communicate in the world shaped by business and government?

One of the visitors listened intently, asked a few more questions about Amira's children, and then made an offer: "Would you be willing for Happy and Hannatu to take extra classes after school with us? We would provide them with a meal and all the materials they need. The educational center will be right here in the village, so it won't be dangerous to walk there." Amira didn't answer right away. She could tell the missionary was trying to calm all her fears before she could even voice them. "In fact, if you'll come with me, I can walk you to where we hope to break ground."

The students gathered around the stage. It was the Sunday after Christmas, and money had been arriving up until the last minute. Would they be able to build an educational center in Nigeria? Christmas Day had passed, and not one kid that morning complained about having fewer gifts. All they wanted to know was whether or not they had made their goal.

"Well, first of all, I want you to know I am so proud of you," their pastor said as he took the stage, pausing to gain his composure. It had been a long month of hoping and praying, and he had been more moved by the efforts of these kids than he had ever dreamed he would be. "We all worked together this month and learned a lot about sacrifice and service. We learned about generosity and blessing. You set an amazing example for the rest of the church . . ."

Now he was drawing the moment out, teasing his audience with the suspense. He knew every kid standing there that day was dying to know—had they done it? Had they reached their goal?

" . . . and so it is my privilege to announce—we break ground on the education center next month! You did it!"

Cheers erupted from the students. Some started jumping up and down, others hugged. Parents stood by on the outskirts, some with their hands over their mouths in surprise. *Our kids really did it!*

Amira walked with the missionary, who spread arms open wide, gesturing at the empty area of dry ground. "It will be called *Igmin Kibe*—Children of the Kingdom. It will be a reminder to the students who walk through the door that they are God's kids. These children—your children—are children of God's kingdom, and he has never forgotten them. They are not alone." The missionary turned and looked straight into Amira's eyes. "You are not alone."

"*Igmin Kibe will* be the name of the center," the pastor explained. "It's a phrase in the local dialect, which means 'children of the kingdom'—God's kids. For me that name holds double meaning. Yes, those children in Nigeria are in God's kingdom. I hope they see the sign and know God is watching out for them. But I see our children here, and how God used them to send a powerful message—a message I hope they know for themselves. They are not alone." He looked down at the hopeful faces gathered around the stage. "You are *igmin kibe*."

It took a year for the construction to be completed. But on January 10, 2011, the Igmin Kibe Education Center was dedicated, and classes officially started on January 24. The first day, only ten students entered—they were between the ages of seven and ten. The small numbers allowed the

POST CARD

CORRESPONDENCE

Igmin kibe means "children of the kingdom" in the language that is spoken in Happy's village. This dialect is called Rukuba. There are around 500 different active languages in Nigeria.

teachers to focus on each child's individual and immediate needs.

The students were children of families who had lost one or more parents, and they walked together from the Kisayhip village. Leading the line around the rocks, over the small hill, and across the field, was Happy.

Happy and her sister Hannatu were among the ten kids Back2Back invited to that first class. Happy's first teacher said about her, "Happy is the type of person

One day some parents brought their children to Jesus so he could touch and bless them. But the disciples scolded the parents for bothering him.

When Jesus saw what was happening, he was angry with his disciples. He said to them, "Let the children come to me. Don't stop them! For the Kingdom of God belongs to those who are like these children. I tell you the truth, anyone who doesn't receive the Kingdom of God like a child will never enter it."

—Mark 10:13-15 (NLT)

Igmin Kibe Education Center

that, if you met her outside of the village, you would have no idea what she goes home to each night. She is so content with what she has and has an amazing positive attitude. She loves to show affection and express her love for those around her (which is rare in this culture). One of my favorite memories of Happy is one day when I was in the classroom after school working on lesson plans. The kids didn't want to go home, so they came in the room and were just sitting around. All of a sudden, Happy starts spinning around the room and singing 'If You're Happy and You Know It.' This is a song we sang daily in class, but I didn't know if Happy was catching onto the words. Well, it turns out, she knew every word! She gleefully started leading the other students around the room while dancing and singing the song. I thought this was a very fitting thing for *Happy* to do."

~~~~~~~~~~~~~~~~~~

Happy's life has transformed since joining the Back2Back orphan care program. I (Beth) saw her this last year, and she pulled me into a room to read me a long book in English. I heard confidence in her voice and saw how proud she was of what she has been learning. She has a wonderful teacher, Esther, who has been a great mentor to Happy in spiritual truths. Esther is always opening her Bible and teaching

Esther and her students at the center

Happy reads to Beth.

God's Word. She is the answer to many people's prayers for consistent, capable, godly adults to enter into these children's lives.

When I asked Happy about her home, she told me she was obedient and a help to her mom. She said she was the only one who could really make her mother laugh! Happy was working hard at school, making plans for her future (she said she wants to be a doctor!), and trusting in the God who has never left her alone.

In Nigerian rural areas, about 1 in 3 persons is without a job. Back2Back Ministries works together with Nigerian communities to create sustainable income sources and to bring hope to kids through education.

Chase loves to hear reports on Igmin Kibe. Every time he sees a picture or hears a story, he is filled with a joy that can't compete with anything money has ever bought him. He's not sure when or how, but someday he hopes to travel and meet the children from the village. When he hears about people from somewhere in the world far from him, he remembers that God is always working on their behalf. And now he asks God more regularly, "How do you want to use me?" However God will answer and wherever Chase's faith will take him, he is certain of these truths:

God sees him.
God listens to him.
God is coming for him.
God will never leave him.
God has a plan.

Back2Back has moved Happy now to a new school, outside of the village, where she can continue on with what she's been learning in the education center. She had to repeat the fourth grade, which was hard for her in the beginning. At first the new school was a challenge, but she has made a huge improvement—raising her overall percentage by 13 percent this year.

REMEMBER THIS

Everyone involved in this story was sure that God had orchestrated this gift of the education center. He had used his body of believers to do so, as he heard the cries of the widows. God answered them powerfully: *I am your Father. I do hear you. You are not alone.* But he also gave them the strength to be a part of the answer—he moved mothers like Amira to encourage their children, to trust in the plan God had for them. And he moved the children of the middle school ministry to give more than they thought they could to build hope in a place they might never see.

Everyone has a part in God's stories. Everyone has something to give, and a way they can serve. No gift is too small. Like the widow Jesus observed, who came and placed her very small coins in the offering, we all have the opportunity to hand over to God everything we have—and watch him give us more than we could imagine. The heart of the Igmin Kibe center is that students would learn and grow and become stronger, but more importantly, that they would gain a better understanding of who they are—and what they have to offer—as children of the Most High King.

I am confident that, as challenges come Happy's way in the future, she will remember the early lessons God taught her.

He sees us.

He listens.

He comes for us.

He never leaves us.

He has a plan.

Happy became stronger through working at hard things. As she continues to learn, do you think she will become stronger? Why? Do you think Chase and his friends became stronger through working to meet their goal? Think about a goal that matters a lot to you. What kind of work will you have to do to meet your goal?

Paul writes to the Thessalonians: "So encourage each other and build each other up, just as you are already doing. Dear brothers and sisters, honor those who are your leaders in the Lord's work. They work hard among you and give you spiritual guidance. Show them great respect and wholehearted love because of their work" (1 Thessalonians 5:11-13, NLT). Who do you know who works hard for God? How can encouraging others and giving guidance sometimes be hard work? How can you do the Lord's work this week?

Chapter 4

TANYA'S VOICE

I (Beth) sat spellbound in my seat. A young Ukrainian girl stood bravely on the stage and closed her eyes. Soon her voice filled the large Atlanta conference room, as she sang a song to Jesus with her whole heart. Blonde curls fell around her face, and her accent bore witness that this story we were seeing had not been unfolding in this country for very long. She finished singing and nodded her head to the audience. The applause was thunderous. I looked around the room and saw many people wiping away tears.

I wanted to know more about her, so I waited patiently in line for my turn to meet this remarkable young woman. Questions filled my mind. *Where is she from? How did she get here? What's her story?*

Finally I got my chance to find out more. "My name is Beth, and it's a pleasure to meet you." She smiled at me confidently, no doubt encouraged by the crowd's reaction to her gift. "You were amazing. Thanks for singing to us tonight." She thanked me in turn, and I continued, "I have been sharing for a while about the God who writes our stories. I can see a God-story in you, and I am dying to hear it. Would you be willing to share? Do you see him as the author of your story?"

"Oh, yes!" Her answer came swiftly. Then she giggled for a minute, hands covering her face. "How else can you explain . . . how should I call it? Well . . . all this." Her hands spread wide—she gestured to the room, the stage, and back to a woman looking at me over her shoulder.

Encouraged by her response, I asked, "Will you tell me, slowly? How did it start? When did you know God was doing something extraordinary for you?"

Her eyes twinkled, and she broke out into a wide grin. "This is my favorite part, telling how God came for me . . ."

I pulled up a chair, and she started from the beginning.

Tanya was just a little girl when she lost her father—her *bat'ko*. She remembers him as hardworking and kind—working with her grandfather, who was a doctor. When Tanya was born, her *matir* said that her father had thrown rocks at the hospital window

Bat'ko means "father."
Matir means "mother."
Ukrainian is a language with a very different alphabet from English. Ukrainian words in this story are written so you can have an idea of how the words might sound.

and brought them flowers. At that time in Ukraine, fathers were not allowed in the hospital to be with the mothers when they had their babies.

She had always been told that her father was happy to have a baby girl.

After losing him, Tanya's single mother cared for her as well as she could, for as long as she could. But several years later, Tanya's mother passed away as well, leaving the girl with few choices.

Life before this loss was marked by happy images—a carefree little girl playing with her cousins and climbing apple trees. Once she had climbed high in a tree and then fallen from a branch—landing so hard on her feet that she had fractured them. But she laughed as she told me about her injury. "I always know now when it's going to rain—my feet are better than a meteorologist." She paused and looked down at the tips of her shiny black shoes. "It's just my little reminder that I sometimes go too far out on the branch."

She was a little girl with a big spirit and a big heart—she loved being with people. When the closest people in her life were suddenly gone, her world was shattered. Her few things were packed up, and she moved to an orphanage, with an uncertain future ahead of her.

A few years passed. Tanya became settled into the routines of her new home. Sometimes she remembered glimpses of her life before, and she missed her family—the cousins she used to play with, and especially her mother's face.

An apple tree in a misty Ukrainian field.

One day in the middle of a brutal Ukrainian winter, ice covered the ground and a big snow blanketed the country. Tanya and a friend stood looking out a frost-covered window in the room they shared with several others. Huge snowflakes fell before their eyes. Tanya remembered noticing how each one was different. As the girls watched the beautiful snow, they noticed three cars making their way slowly down the long lane to the orphanage—the cars seemed to creep along in an effort not to skate off the road.

The girls were immediately curious. Who was coming? What did they want? News spread fast around the orphanage as others witnessed the same scene. Everyone was asking questions. Visitors did not come often to the home, so to have three cars arrive all at once seemed a special event.

Andra sat in her Atlanta sunroom, soaking in the warmth of the rays. She stared out the window at the chilly, gray winter day. Though the year was quickly coming to an end, in her heart Andra felt so much was just beginning. God had been moving in her, bringing questions to her mind. The questions had come as she observed friends going through the adoption process. It was a familiar idea—adoption. Even as a child herself, she had dreamed of adopting a child in need of a family. To give a child a home—to share her heart and her family—it all seemed like such a good idea. The best idea.

Since her own family's roots came in part from Eastern Europe, her heart was naturally drawn to that area of the world. She started asking questions on her own: *Is it possible? How would we do it?* Then one day, sitting in the warmth of the sunroom again, she posed the question to her husband, "What would you think about the idea of adopting a child from Ukraine?"

Travis's eyes met his wife's. "I think . . . that's a great idea!"

The couple grew more excited as they began searching together for a child to welcome into their family.

Tanya and her friend heard the director greeting the guests as they climbed out of their cars. The strangers were shown into the front room. The two girls hid within earshot, trying to learn why the visitors had come. They certainly weren't the only children on this spy mission that day. But Tanya's heart thumped a little harder when she heard her name being called.

"Tanya, *pryyikhaty syudy*."

She glanced at her friend in alarm. "Why do you think they are calling your name?" her friend whispered. "Who are they? What do they want?"

Tanya shrugged and raced away down the stairs. She didn't know any more than her friend did, but she wanted to find out.

The director's voice bellowed, loud enough for

everyone to hear, "Tanya, come meet our guests. They want to meet you and interview you."

Interview me? For what? She couldn't imagine how they even knew about her, let alone what they could want with her.

One of the guests was speaking in a language Tanya didn't understand, but from the movies she had seen she knew enough to guess that it was English. Through a translator, the woman addressed Tanya. "We are here visiting, hoping to meet children who might be eligible (and interested) to go on a trip for a few weeks to the United States. Would you like to do something like that?"

Tanya just stared at the woman for a minute,

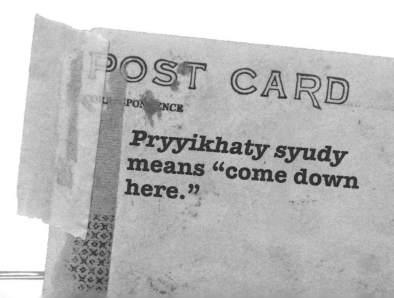

POST CARD

CORRESPONDENCE

Pryyikhaty syudy means "come down here."

trying to register what she was saying. Can you imagine? It was like a dream for her. This was the girl who liked to climb up tall trees. This was the girl whose dreams were far bigger than the story she was living out every day in this small Ukrainian orphanage.

Did she want to go to the United States—to a place she had only seen in the movies and heard about in school?

"Tak!" Tanya nervously answered the rest of the visitors' questions, hoping she was saying what they wanted to hear.

Nothing happened for a few months; then in the spring the director of the orphanage gathered several of the children together to announce that they had been chosen for the hosting program.

POST CARD

Tak means "yes."

We'll be traveling to America in June! Tanya was so excited—at age fifteen, she was ready to have new experiences and meet new people. Life in the orphanage seemed monotonous—every day a repeat of the day before. A future life when she would be released from the orphanage was looming, and she had very little hope to hold onto about what that future looked like. She felt sure that the summer of 2012 was going to be an experience she would remember forever.

New Horizons for Children, Inc. (NHFC) is the largest, faith-based orphan hosting organization in the US. Twice a year—over Christmastime and in the summer—orphaned, school-age children from Eastern Europe are flown to various locations throughout the United States to stay with Christian host families. The children normally stay for about four to five weeks. During that time, the host families help the children learn English and life skills, but most importantly, they provide an example of a healthy family and extend the love of Christ to children who often feel hopeless and unwanted. For more information about hosting or helping this Georgia-based organization, go to NHFC.org.

The departure date finally arrived, and Tanya eagerly boarded the plane with several of her friends from school. Her eyes widened as she painted this memory for me. "Some of us were nervous because

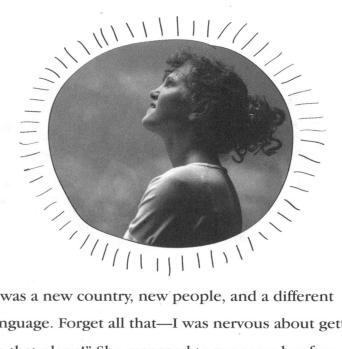

it was a new country, new people, and a different language. Forget all that—I was nervous about getting on that plane!" She managed to suppress her fear enough to walk onboard. They were on a nonstop flight from Kyiv (Kiev), Ukraine, to New York City. There they would spend one night together before going their separate directions to their host families the next morning.

Tanya looked down at the ticket in her hand as she settled into her seat. *Atlanta, Georgia. I hope you are friendly!*

Later in that same summer, Andra and her husband also boarded a flight that would end up in a different country, where a foreign language was spoken. The woman felt the nerves tumbling in her stomach as she glanced at the itinerary in her hand: "Kyiv, Ukraine."

After an uneventful flight, they arrived in the capital city of Ukraine and attended to the rest of their travel arrangements. They had a long trip ahead—both geographically and emotionally—as they journeyed to the region where an eleven-year-old girl was waiting for them.

They had traveled all this way from the United States to adopt the girl. However, they had been warned that this adoption could end up being particularly challenging due to some details about the orphanage where she lived. They were not afraid. They felt called to pursue the adoption and were determined to face the challenges head-on.

On the long flight to the States, Tanya was a curious observer of her fellow travelers. She noticed several Americans who seemed very kind. Someone spilled a drink near her seat, and several people piped up with voices of assurance: "It's OK—don't worry!"

Tanya was not used to that. "People didn't talk to

each other like that where I was from." She hoped all the Americans she would meet would be as nice as those on the flight. Her mind turned again to wondering what her host family would be like.

After what seemed like a hundred hours, the couple finally arrived at the orphanage. They were excited to meet their potential daughter face-to-face. But there was a problem. Through an interpreter they understood that forces out of the girl's control had made it impossible for her to go through with the adoption.

Travis and Andra were devastated. They asked questions and pushed for information, but in the end one thing was clear. They would be going home again. Without a daughter.

It was the worst news they could imagine hearing at that moment.

Tanya's host family picked her up the following day as scheduled, and they took her right away to a Russian grocery store. They had been learning what foods were typically eaten in Ukraine, and the host mother, Andrea, wanted Tanya to choose foods that would feel familiar to her. To Tanya it was yet another example of kindness, and she thought it was a good sign. Even though she was exhausted from the flight and all the excitement, she tried to remember every detail as they drove to her new home. She wanted to be able to tell her friends back in Ukraine all about her experiences once she returned there.

Among other outings, Tanya's host family took her shopping for new clothes that would suit the hot, humid summer days of Atlanta better. And Tanya quickly learned to use the computer to translate everything she wanted to say.

From Beth's Journal

Disappointment. That knot in your stomach that twists up when all your plans have come crashing down. You prayed, you listened, you followed—but now what? No one seeks to be disappointed, but I can look back and be amazed about the many times I've encountered God's overwhelming love when I've felt the most crushed. When my plans fall apart, I see how the path he has woven for me has never been broken. When what I've depended on crumbles, I can finally lay down on the solid truth that he is always there for me. God, I pray you help me to keep stretching and asking and trying to get to the places where I know I'm weak, and your love is so strong.

She felt an immediate connection with the young children in the family. It was easy to be with them and play with them. Tanya was happy and eager to learn about her new friends and what life was like in this city called Atlanta. So far, this hosting arrangement was turning out *exactly* as she had hoped.

But there was something else too—something working in Tanya's heart. She had never really considered being adopted before. She knew some kids in her orphanage who really longed for it, but to her it just had never seemed to be a possibility, so she had put it out of her mind. Maybe it was because she still had memories of her own family, or maybe it was because she had an independent streak. Or maybe it was just because she knew older kids like her had

POST CARD

CORRESPONDENCE

Dodomu means "home."

very little chance of ever being taken in by a family. Who knows? Tanya herself wasn't even sure. But for whatever reason, up until that time she had rejected the idea of being adopted.

Now, sitting down with this family to eat dinner together, going shopping together, taking drives together—it all felt so right. So good. It felt like *dodomu*. And Tanya started wondering if there had been something more missing from her life than what she realized.

The husband and wife retraced their path back to the busy city of Kyiv. They had followed their heavenly Father to places they never even knew existed before, only to find the door closed. *What do we do now? Do we just go home?* It seemed impossible—to return home without a child. They had felt led to come, and led to adopt. They had so much they wanted to give to a child. But if they wanted to pursue another adoption, it would mean completely starting the process over.

With extremely heavy hearts they returned to their hotel in Kyiv. Andra sat on the edge of the bed and stared off into space, looking for answers that were not there. They both felt so confused and clueless as to what their next steps should be. Travis came and sat beside his wife, and they prayed together, asking God to show them what to do.

Kyiv (or Kiev) is the capital city of Ukraine. It is one of the oldest cities in Eastern Europe, and is considered the birthplace of the Russian Orthodox Church.

Tanya's sixteenth birthday fell on one of the last days of her visit in Atlanta. It was bittersweet. She was excited about being a year older, about getting presents, and about the party the host family had planned for her. Together they had picked out a huge cake, and the family had invited many people to celebrate her life. She had a lot to look forward to that day, and she definitely felt special. However, turning sixteen also marked another milestone for her—it was the time when she would no longer be eligible to be adopted. She would "age out" of the orphan care system

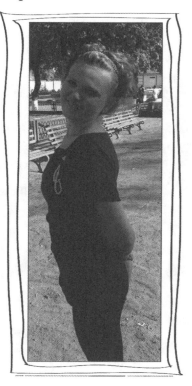

and would be largely on her own soon after her return to Ukraine. Her hope for a permanent family would die on this day.

As she sat on her bed in this home that had become so familiar, and images of her time with this family flashed through her mind, she couldn't help feeling sad. *Being in a family wouldn't be such a bad idea after all*, she thought. *If only I had more time.*

Less than twenty-four hours after their return from the orphanage where their adoption had failed, Andra's phone began to be inundated with messages from several friends in the States. The messages all said the same thing: "There is a lovely Ukrainian teenage girl being hosted by Andrea's family who desires to be adopted. Only problem is, she will age out . . . today."

This was exciting news! Because of the unique timing, and because they were still in Ukraine, the couple had a feeling that God was moving in this story, but there were still lots of questions to be asked and answered.

During the party, Tanya noticed the adults talking about something. They seemed serious, and the long looks in her direction made her think they must be talking about her, but she couldn't hear or understand everything they were saying. She went on enjoying the party and her friends, and didn't think much about it.

Then Andrea, Tanya's host mother, called her into the house. She had her sit by the computer so they could use it to translate their conversation back and forth.

"Princess T, I have a question. I know this question will feel big and I don't ask it lightly, so take your time answering." Her voice quivered a little, and Tanya felt a chill go through her body. "You and I both know today is the last day you can be adopted into a family. I have a friend *right now* who is in Ukraine, trying to adopt, and she is wondering . . . would you like to be in her family?"

It was clear Tanya didn't know how to answer—stress and fear mingled with excitement as thoughts went running through her mind. It was such a shock, and she needed to think. But there was so little time!

Andrea told her she could think about it overnight and talk to her in the morning.

Tanya spent her birthday night at a friend's house and dreamed about what it would be like to live right here, in the United States. And what it would be like to be part of a family.

Under the pressure of time, the couple thought through the new situation that had come to them. Andra knew the host mother, Andrea. But Andrea hadn't even known they were in Ukraine—or that they were trying to adopt—until some mutual friends relayed that message. Then Andrea and the couple started communicating back and forth. Andrea was able to answer some of their questions, but there were still more.

In various ways, they were not sure they were prepared to adopt a sixteen-year-old. Their current paperwork had only been approved for a child up to the age of fifteen. Could they get their documents amended in time? Would the adoption even be legally possible?

And what about the girl? Sixteen was a lot different from eleven. What if she wasn't certain? What if she changed her mind? Neither of them was sure they could handle another disappointment. Was it too much to do? Or was it too much to give up? How could they decide?

Tanya and her potential new parents communicated via Skype. Again, Tanya felt that this family seemed very nice. But she also wanted to talk to someone from her life back home—someone who could understand her voice, hear her concerns, and help her with this huge decision. She was anxious and eager as she connected with one of her cousins in Ukraine. He was the same age, and she had known him her whole life. She quickly laid the situation out for him and asked his advice.

"In my opinion, if you say yes, you are making the right decision. This will give you a better life," he said, looking straight into the lens. "If you come back here and go out from the orphanage, you will just work your whole life. I know I will miss you—but it's not about me, it's about you."

Her cousin was a Christian, and Tanya knew he loved her with a sacrificial love. Later as she looked back on this story, she could see how God used him to encourage her.

She ended the Skype call and sat there for a moment. This was a higher branch than she had ever climbed to, and she felt like she was walking far out on this limb. But God had given her an adventurous spirit and a longing for more.

She said yes.

It had been an amazing, frustrating, wearying couple of days. They had been asking God so many questions. Now they asked, "Is this our child?" And they knew somewhere across an ocean, a girl was asking, "God, are these my parents?"

Somehow, all the necessary pieces of information fell together. And the pieces of their hearts also fell into place.

And they said yes.

Tanya's host family drove her by the house where her new family lived. It was so close to where she had been living, she couldn't believe it. She got out of the car and looked around the yard, even peeked in

the windows. Andrea had told her the couple had a pool, so Tanya circled the house, asking in her heavily accented English, "Where is the pool?" Andrea could see that Tanya was trying to imagine herself living here, coming home to this place.

"It seemed like a nice home—such a cute lawn!— a place where a nice family would live, where a God I hardly knew might have a story for me," Tanya recalled, as she continued telling me her story. She gathered as much information as she could. She checked out the trees and looked around at the neighbors.

I think I can do this. I want to do this. Yes, let's do this, she told herself. *I think this could be good. And if not, there's always the pool.* She smiled. It all seemed like a dream.

As they drove away from the neighborhood, Tanya peppered Andrea as best as she could with questions of a more practical nature. Some questions and answers they worked out later with the help of the translating software. "Will I go back and say *do pobachennya* to my friends? Will I still see you after the adoption? Do you think I can learn English?"

Andrea was patient with Tanya, but she was excited too. This was a big story, and she knew (and Tanya would later come to understand) no one could have orchestrated it but God.

POST CARD

Do pobachennya means "good-bye."

Monday was Tanya's birthday. Tanya and Andrea visited the family's house on Tuesday. And on Wednesday they connected with the family again via Skype. By Thursday, fear had set in for both Tanya and her potential new parents. Their main worries were similar: Will she change her mind? Will they follow through? There is an enemy who seeks to hurt children and divide families, and he was whispering a song of heartache and disappointment to both Tanya and her would-be mom. But many were praying for these hearts, and God was battling for them both—protecting their minds and defeating their fears.

Tanya remembered the words she kept saying to herself: *I will trust her. She says she is coming for me. I will believe her.* "When I didn't have faith of my own, God gave it to me," Tanya recalled.

Tanya boarded a plane once again and returned to the orphanage and school in Ukraine. She waited for strangers, not knowing for sure that they would come. And her hopeful mom and dad returned to the offices of children's services in Ukraine to complete all the relevant documentation—all the while praying that Tanya wouldn't change her mind.

"I laugh now—we both wanted each other so much and couldn't even see each other, let alone say it to each other," Tanya said.

It was a beautiful morning on August 13, 2012. It was also a morning heavy with trepidation, excitement, and cautious optimism, among many other emotions. It was time for the couple to pick up their daughter and bring her home.

The pair arrived at Balta Orphanage 2, papers in hand, and stood in the hall outside the director's door with their attorney, the translator, and a social worker.

Today is the big day.

Tanya was washing her clothes in the sink, as the kids there often did. Her friend asked, "When do you think they'll come for you? Or do you think you'll still be here in two years . . . washing your clothes in the sink with all the rest of us?" She had been asked some version of those same questions a hundred times since she'd returned. The others in the home had heard someone was coming for her, but everyone knew that Tanya was already sixteen. They questioned, "Who adopts someone that old?"

As she wrung the water from her sweater, Tanya looked up at the mirror and caught a glimpse of some faces she didn't recognize coming around the corner.

Could it be?

She hadn't heard from her soon-to-be parents in a few weeks, and despite her brave assurances to others that they would come, she admitted now that she had started to wonder.

But as the features of her new mother's face appeared in the mirror, she dropped the soggy sweater and spun around.

"My mama and papa are here!" And without hesitation, she jumped right into their arms.

Tanya's mother put her hand on her daughter's shoulder and finished the story. "I can remember every detail of that moment. My eyes connected with a set of beautiful blue eyes in the mirror of that bathroom, where a precious girl was washing clothes in the sink. In that millisecond of time, our hearts connected and we realized who we each were looking at. I heard her scream, and she came running into our arms. And in that moment, all was made right. All was made clear."

It had been ten weeks since they first left their home to complete their adoption process. At one point, nothing had made sense—not why they heard the call to come, not why the other girl changed her mind, not why, even after their disappointment, they still felt compelled to stay.

Still somewhat in shock at the turn of events, the mother felt a peace she knew didn't come from herself. This girl, unplanned for by them, was totally planned for by Jesus. As Tanya jumped into her arms, her thoughts echoed Tanya's voice from the beginning of this story: *How else can you explain . . . all this?*

Tanya says a final farewell to her home of nine years.

On September 22, Tanya Isabelle said good-bye to her homeland. She boarded a plane bound for the States for the second time that year, but on this flight, she sat next to her mom and pops. That night she slept in a soft bed inside the house that she had peeped into just a couple months before.

That fall, she started high school. The first year held some challenges: she was homesick for her cousins and other extended family, she didn't know much English, she didn't have friends, and school was hard. There were so many adjustments that had to be made. But after the first year, things became easier for her (and her family). As her language improved, so did everything else. She met more friends and got involved in after-school activities. She walked into church and into a community who delighted in her story.

She has grown to understand her Storyweaver as her Savior and prays every day to him, thanking him for this chapter she is now living. In her own words, "I love to study the Bible and sing worship music because it is all about God. He changed my whole life in a very good way. If I did not know him, I might not

Tanya and Andra (in matching pajamas) talk on Skype to friends.

REMEMBER THIS

have experienced what I am living right now. He opened my heart to him, and I now love him with all my heart."

Today, at nineteen, Tanya loves American music, watching movies, and eating pizza. By the time this book is published, she will be attending college, and she sometimes dreams of becoming an international flight attendant and seeing the world. She connects with friends in Ukraine and shares her life and story with people in both countries. And she loves telling how God came for her—at just the right time.

Think about Tanya's story. What kinds of things did the characters in this story give? Have you ever felt God asking you to give in a big way? What happened?

Matthew 25 includes a story Jesus told about three servants. At the end of the story, in verse 29 (NLT), the master says, "To those who use well what they are given, even more will be given, and they will have an abundance. But from those who do nothing, even what little they have will be taken away." Read the whole story if you have time. What do you think Jesus meant by saying these words?

Chapter 5
MARIO'S STEPS

"Mamá, a dónde vas?"

Mario was only three years old when his mom left. Before she left, there was constant fighting and a feeling of chaos in the house. That was all he could remember. The fighting felt normal to him—it was all he'd ever known since he was born. After his mother left, the stillness in the house was louder than any fight he'd ever heard.

"Papi, I'm hungry."

"Papi, when will you be back?"

"Papi, my stomach hurts."

The needs and complaints of a toddler can be relentless, and Mario was no exception. He missed his mom and felt insecure when his dad left the room, much less the house. He looked for reasons to ask his dad for help, just so he could be comforted.

Papi, Papi, Papi. All the questions gave the weary man a headache. Every moment since the children's mother left, he had faced their little voices, constantly asking for something. He did not blame them. He knew they were hungry much of the time, and scared. But he also didn't know how to comfort them.

When she walked out, and every minute after, he had thought about following her. He wanted her to know how the children missed her—how he missed her. He wanted to make things better. But what use would it be to find her and bring her back to a place she didn't want to be?

All he knew for certain was that he had to keep working. If he didn't work, no one would eat.

POST CARD

CORRESPONDENCE

Mamá, a dónde vas? means "Mama, where are you going?" A dónde vamos? means "Where are we going?" Accent marks—those little lines over letters— in Spanish are used to show which syllable gets stressed in a word or to distinguish two words that are otherwise spelled alike.

Mario's sister tried her best to take care of her little brother, but she was only two years older. She wasn't sure how to make meals, or what time they should go to bed, or what to do about a stomachache. She tried hard to amuse her brother—making up little games for them to play with pebbles or making a ball out of wadded up clothing. They obeyed their father's warnings about staying inside and out of trouble.

To them it always seemed like their dad was gone forever—he worked long hours. Many nights they held each other and cried themselves to sleep while they waited for their father to come home from work.

It was clear—there was no question in his mind. He touched the tear-stained cheek of his sleeping daughter and listened to her breathing, punctuated still by the little gasps that told him her sobs hadn't stopped very long ago. Her arms curled around her brother's head on the mat, as if she was protecting him, even in sleep. It had been two years since their mom had left. *I can't do this anymore*, he thought. He put his head in his hands and rubbed his tired eyes. *I can't do this to them.* He knew what he had to do. It was about the only thing that was clear to him just now.

"*A dónde vamos?*" Mario's sister asked.

"We are going to go somewhere where they can take care of you while I work."

Her eyes widened. "Then we will come home with you at night?"

"No, you'll stay there at night too," he said, trying to keep his tone steady. He saw the tears start to fill her eyes, and he added quickly, "But I will come and visit you—every weekend, if they let me."

Mario was listening—not just to the words, but to the quiver in his father's voice and the panic in his sister's questions. *What is wrong?* he wondered. It was clear something was not right, but he didn't understand everything his father was saying—or what it could possibly mean for the rest of his life.

"Here we are." His dad paid the taxi driver, and they lingered for a while near a gate. No one said another word. Then his dad led them by the hand into a building and had them sit down on some chairs.

The next couple of minutes were the most painful of Mario's life. Worse than when his mother left—that was all a sad blur to him. He had been so little then—he couldn't even really remember her face. But when his dad walked away . . . Mario had no words for it. It was as if his heart were being ripped out of his chest. He saw his father's shoulders shaking, and watched his hand go up to his face in a familiar motion—rubbing his eyes. He wanted to run after him, but someone held him back. And if that wasn't bad enough, another stranger came in and took his sister's hand, dragging them apart.

He screamed for the next hour until finally worn out; then he curled up on the bench in the office. *Where am I? What is this place?* he wondered, just before his eyes closed.

He woke up as he was being carried into a dorm

room full of beds and placed on a blue comforter. He wasn't sleeping anymore, but he pretended that he was, opening his eyes very slightly so he could see around the room. He spotted a closet full of clothes and a table that had some food left over from a previous meal.

He was aching and not sure what to do about it. It was hard to know where the aches were coming from. Was it hunger? fatigue? sickness? He didn't even know how to say what he was feeling, or who here in the room would care to listen.

If he could have talked to someone in that moment, he would have told them he was hurting from too much sadness.

A woman, whom he later found out was called Lorena, let him sleep through the evening and then the night. She came over to the bed and slipped off his shoes and covered him up. He still laid there, eyes shut, playing a game of if-I-can't-see-you-then-you-can't-see-me.

The man shut his eyes tight—trying to block out the memory of his children's scared faces. But it was no use. He couldn't sleep. But he had to rest. He had to get back to his work in a few hours, and if he wasn't alert, he would make mistakes. He could not afford to lose his job. Then he would have nothing—and nothing to offer his children. He turned over and tried to think of happier times. He imagined his children waking up to a good, warm breakfast. *Mario will love that!* As he dreamed of his children receiving comfort, he drifted off to sleep.

By the morning, the hunger in Mario's belly was louder than the ache in his heart. He woke to the sound of the other boys getting up. Mario watched as the boys showered and got dressed and tidied up their room. Since he was still wearing the same clothes he had arrived in, he just slipped on his shoes and followed the boys as they lined up for what Mario hoped was breakfast.

"This is our table." One of the other boys showed him where to get his eggs and sit down. Mario looked around the *comedor* for his sister. He finally caught sight of her, sitting with more strangers. The aching twist in his stomach returned. But then he waved to her and she waved back to him, and he felt a little better.

Later, Mario talked to his sister at recess at their new school. Mario was in kindergarten, and his sister was in second grade. That meant they would get to walk together to school in the morning, but then they would come home at different times. As his sister explained the details of their schedules, Mario felt his stomach twisting again. New routines made him feel anxious and insecure.

POST CARD

CORRESPONDENCE

Comedor means "dining room" or "dining hall."

In the children's home, all the kids ate together in a large room.

His sister saw his brow furrow and patted his hand. "Don't worry, Mario, we will get used to it here—you will get the hang of it, you'll see. These people are nice, and they want to help us. Plus, on Sunday we'll get to see Papi."

Mario's face brightened up immediately at this news. The rest of the day went by quickly—there was so much to learn and do. That evening he gathered with the other boys as Lorena read them a story about a boy who threw a stone at a giant. She prayed over the boys and then helped them get tucked into their beds.

"Only two more sleeps until my dad comes to visit," Mario told Lorena confidently, as she straightened out his blanket.

"That's right. I hope you get to see him." She chose her words carefully. She had comforted many a child in her time at the children's home who never received visitors—even though each time they expected someone to come. She knew better than to contribute to a false hope. But she smiled at Mario,

Minimum wage in Mexico is equal to around $4 an hour. At that rate, a person living with 2 children would be making less than ½ of what is considered poverty level income in the United States.

asking God silently to help his father be able to come. Mario snuggled down into his bed and imagined how he would play on Sunday with his dad and what he could show him. He wondered if there was anything he could do or say that would make his father bring them back home.

As he pushed the gate open, Mario's dad took a deep breath. He had worried all the way there about how his children would handle this visit. Would they be happy to see him? Would they be angry? He hoped they wouldn't cry. And he hoped they would tell him the people there had been nice to them. But mostly he worried about how he would leave them again. The thought of making them sad almost kept him from coming. But he had to come. He had to see their faces. He missed them so much. He wanted them to know how much he loved them.

Lorena was relieved to see that Mario's father did come on Sunday. He came that Sunday and nearly every Sunday after that. Each time, the children ran to hug him. Mario's sister talked fast, telling everything that had happened in her week. Mario tugged on his father's arm, wanting to show him where they played and get his dad to kick the ball around with him.

But no matter how nice a visit they had together, their good-byes were always pretty terrible. As the minutes of the visit came to an end, Mario would ask again, "When can we come home?"

The question made him wince. He knew his children were receiving good care here at the children's home. They were safe and clean and well fed. A month or more had gone by, and they were getting used to their new routines. He could tell they felt settled there. They were making new friends. And they always had someone with them—they were never left alone. He was sure this was the best solution for a family with no mother.

"Not yet, son," he answered again. It was his standard reply. "But maybe someday . . ."

Growing up without a mother left a hole in Mario's heart. And as he got older, he could feel this hole filling with anger, sadness, and distrust. He constantly questioned and challenged the adults in his life, and he clung to his father during his visits. His emotions were strong and could change quickly. He was easily riled and became immediately tearful when a situation wasn't going as we wished.

His mom visited just twice during the time Mario was in kindergarten to sixth grade. They were quick visits—answering none of Mario's questions. It was a bittersweet reminder of a woman he was connected to by blood, yet had no real relationship with.

Mario tried to fill up this hole in his life in better ways. He tried to stay busy, playing with friends and enjoying the field trips provided by visiting mission teams—anything to distract him from thinking about his mom and the way she walked out on him and his

sister. But then he would see other moms visit and feel sad all over again.

Sometimes when he was sick or in a special school program, he wondered what it would be like to be able to share those moments with his mom. What would she do to make him feel better? Would she be proud of him when he performed well? But these joined the long list of questions he had that just went unanswered.

He stuffed the disappointment and sorrow and anger and hurt under the surface, and tried not to let it out. Most days he succeeded—no one saw a sign of what was going on inside him. But he knew those feelings were always there and could be provoked in unexpected moments.

Mario finished elementary school and went on to junior high. There he felt his heart change again. For a time, he lost interest in seeing his mom, and he grew to respect the faithful commitment his dad had always shown. One Sunday, his father said, "You know, son, when you finish junior high, you can come back home and live with me. You can get a job at a factory or a construction site." He looked hopefully at Mario.

Mario couldn't believe it. He had been waiting what seemed like his whole life for this moment—for his dad to finally answer his question, "When can we come home?"

But Mario felt confused. He hung his head. "Dad, I don't know. Of course I want to come home with you. I've always wanted to come home with you. But they are talking to me here about a program where I could go on and study more school, all the way through college if I want. I know I am smart, and I can work hard, but I don't know. Do you think it's a good idea? It would mean not moving home with you."

"No, son, it would mean a whole lot more. It would mean a future for you. It would mean a different kind of life. I want you to fight for your dreams." He reached over and placed his weathered hand, calloused from the years he had served as a gardener, on Mario's. "I will keep coming. No one can stop me. You lean forward. Take the right steps. Follow your dream."

I don't have any dreams, Mario thought. "OK, Papa, I will go, but it feels like I am leaving you all over again." Mario's eyes filled with tears, and the rest of the day they talked about anything and everything else besides the future.

~~~~~~~~~~~~~~~~

THE HOPE PROGRAM

Through the Hope Program, Back2Back Ministries offers orphans and vulnerable children an opportunity to pursue their educational goals and break the cycle of poverty. Living in a family-style setting, students are mentored, supported through scholarships and tutoring, and encouraged to pursue their dreams. Following Paul's teaching, who was delighted to share not only the gospel, but his life as well (1 Thessalonians 2:8), the goal with each child is for them to become dependent on the Lord, interdependent in their community, and independent, self-sustaining individuals who give back to their community.

In the end, Mario did choose to enter the Hope Program, more to be near his sister who was already enrolled than to follow any dream. He moved onto campus, bringing along with him all the hate he felt toward his mother and none of the hope he was supposed to have about his future.

But in the summer of 2010, something started to change inside Mario. He went to a retreat, and it felt like the speakers were talking directly to him. They were talking about forgiveness and perseverance. He had never considered the idea that he could be free from this emotional weight he had carried around for so long. What had happened had happened. His mother had left. He couldn't change that, and so he felt like he couldn't change anything—not the ache inside or the anger he held onto or the hurt. But as he listened to these speakers, he realized that maybe there was something he could do. His lack of *la misericordia* had been bringing pain to his life for a long time. *Am I doing this to myself? Is there a way I can feel differently, even without her? God, if you really exist, show me. Prove it by doing something in my life.*

POST CARD

La misericordia means "forgiveness."

One of the leaders prayed for him that weekend and whispered, "God has not left you. Open your heart to God, and it will be different from this point forward." When he finished praying, Mario felt an overwhelming sense of God's presence. He knew he had had a real encounter with God. *Will everything change now?*

It wasn't long before old feelings about his mom came flooding back, and Mario's trust in God shifted with those feelings. On top of that, one of his houseparents in the Hope Program developed cancer, and had to leave for treatment. Mario's anger issues surfaced again, and this time he knew who to direct them toward. He shouted at God, "Why do people I care about always leave?"

Mario's dad kept visiting his son as much as he could. But he could tell Mario was having a hard time. They talked, but often Mario avoided questions that had to do with how he was feeling. He kept talking about all the things he was doing instead.

His dad worried about him. He was not sure how to help Mario, but he found himself mouthing the words, "Please God, comfort my son."

Mario started to withdraw from everyone, spending more and more time alone. His behavior became uncontrollable, and he hurt everyone in his path. He was vomiting the things he wished he could say to his mom on others. He yelled and acted in rage. It reached a point when he had to decide: Would he work through his feelings? Or would he jeopardize his future with his poor choices?

For the next year, Mario went to counseling and talked about his childhood, his anger, his questions. He prayed to God, asking what God had for his life. *Never mind my dreams, Lord. What are your dreams for me? Show me. Then show me how. Show me the steps I need to take.*

Slowly, he realized he did not want to hate his mom anymore. It was too hard and took too much from him. Early in 2013, God spoke to him while on a mission trip to another city. Watching other orphans younger than him wrestle through the same story lines created in him an empathy and a desire to serve children who were living through the same

From Beth's Journal

When we are angry, we are really afraid. That's true not just for orphans, but for you and me too. When someone can't express their fear, it bottles up and spills over in anger or aggression. One of the ways we can serve one another is not to react to someone else's anger, but to listen to God's wisdom in Proverbs when he says, "A gentle answer turns away wrath" (15:1).

experiences he had had as a kid. God was transforming Mario's thinking, turning his thoughts toward others instead of focusing on himself. He returned home from that experience feeling more positive, calm, and focused

than he had felt in a long time. He had begun to take the right steps, now he just needed to stay on the right path.

Not long after the trip, at church one Sunday, his pastor spoke about forgiveness—a theme that kept resurfacing in his life. As the pastor spoke, Mario kept thinking about his mom. When the time came for people who wanted to receive prayer or make a commitment to God to come up to the front, Mario's feet carried him there. He was crying and praying really hard. *I want to be OK. I want to be happy. I want to do things your way, Lord. Quiero ser libre.* He had taken another big step, but he still had a long climb ahead.

A few days later, Mario was alone with God in his thoughts, and felt the Lord pointing out how many people were supporting him in this journey. But in the end, he alone had to decide. He asked God, "What do I need to do to be better?"

The answer came to his mind and heart quickly. *You need to forgive your mom. Not forgiving her holds you back. You need healing in your heart.*

He had known for a while where his mother was living and how to reach her. Finally, he gathered his courage and called her. It was a moment he would never forget.

POST CARD

PONDENCE

Quiero ser libre means "I want to be free."

"*Hola?*"

When she answered, Mario started to cry. He couldn't believe he was actually going to talk with her. "It's Mario. I want to see you."

There was a pause. "Why?" she asked.

"I want to see you."

She didn't ask any more questions this time. "Tell me when and where."

Mario felt instinctively that she was more curious than interested in seeing him, but he didn't care. He gave her directions to a meeting place and told her he would be waiting. After he hung up, he prayed, "God, I'm leaving this all in your hands. Please take control of everything I'm feeling and what I am about to confront."

He took the bus to the train station where they had arranged to meet. He waited eagerly the first hour . . . angrily the second, and depressed the third. *Maybe I have the time wrong?* he thought to himself. *Or maybe she just changed her mind.* By the fourth hour, he had resigned himself to the idea that she wasn't coming at all. He debated the idea of going back, but he didn't want to give up yet. Just as he was starting to lose hope, he saw her.

Even in a crowd of people, even after all this time, he recognized her immediately. Running to her, he threw his arms around her, hugging her and whispering immediately, "I forgive you. I forgive you, Mama. I forgive you for everything that happened between you and Dad. I want to be OK with both of my parents. I need to be. I have to give it up and over to God."

She was clearly shocked. It wasn't the reaction she had been expecting. Both of them were shaking, and they took a seat on a nearby bench. They spoke a long time, not about everything, but about everything that counted. Mario said all the words he needed to say, and as he did, he felt the weight of years of suffering lift off his shoulders.

As he walked home, Mario wondered if his mother would ever meet with him again. Was this just a closing of the past, or was it an opening of the future? Either way, he walked home with a lighter step. His thoughts rose to Heaven. *God, you always have something better for me. Prompting*

Mario and his mom (right).

me to talk to her is a gift you gave her—she's feeling forgiven, like her shame can finally be lifted. And prompting me to talk to her is a gift you gave me— you've given me a freedom I've never had before, a release of anger I thought was just permanently part of who I was. And prompting me to talk to her is a gift you gave my future—I can see ahead now. I can lead others through where I have just been. I still have questions, and I am sure there are doubts that

In Isaiah 6, there's a familiar passage spoken by the prophet that is often quoted in relation to serving in missions: "Here am I. Send me!" But when we read that whole chapter, we see how Isaiah was confronted by an impressive vision which made him feel completely unworthy, even "ruined." Then, in a simple act, God took away his guilt and atoned for his sin. Only after that did Isaiah raise his hand and volunteer to be sent.

What does this mean? Do you have to be sinless to be sent by God? No, Isaiah was still a sinner. But he wasn't burdened by his past anymore—he was set free because God told him he was free. God has those same words for you—will you accept them? Will you let go of your burdens so you can go where God is sending you? "Your guilt is taken away and your sin atoned for" (Isaiah 6:7).

will come in and visit me, but I won't push them—or you!—away any longer. I love this peace. I will fight for it.

"And so, my life has changed since the day I was dropped off at a children's home fifteen years ago," Mario said, as he addressed the crowd gathered in the church. He had felt a desire to share his story—to give hope to others who felt alone. "I continue to visit my mom. We share stories about the seasons we were apart. She is trying to get to know me, and I am trying to get to know her. I can still have moments of confusion or sadness, but now I know what to do. I pray, read the Bible, and serve where I can." He paused and took a deep breath. "In June 2014, I served on a mission trip in Haiti, where I shared my story with the boys who live there. I could tell they were listening, and had lots of questions afterwards for me. Since Haiti, I have been thinking a lot about where God has brought me. I never thought God would take me to a place of healing or use my story to heal others around the world." His voice broke and he struggled for control. "But whatever God says, I want to do; and wherever he sends me, I want to go. My path, the one I must travel, is the journey of a healed heart."

Mario lives in Monterrey, Mexico, where he is finishing up his bachelor's degree in communications. He plans on using his voice to testify to God's pursuit of our broken hearts.

Mario and his sister were sometimes really on their own when their father had to be away at work. But God was still with them. How can you know God is with you, even when you feel all alone?

Mario spent a lot of time feeling angry and lost because he couldn't forgive his mom. Paul wrote to the Colossians and said, "Bear with each other and forgive one another if any of you has a grievance against someone. Forgive as the Lord forgave you" (3:13). How has God forgiven you? What are some things you might need to do to forgive others? Who do you need to go to and either say "I forgive you" or say "I'm sorry"?

Chapter 6

ON EVERY PAGE

Thank you for journeying with me to Haiti, Nigeria, Ukraine, and Mexico. I hope you've learned some new words and met children whose lives teach us more about God. He will never leave us. The Bible teaches about him standing with people in fires and in lions' dens. He has stood with children and beside kings. He loves all the world and is intimately involved in every story you see and hear around you and beyond. He isn't restricted by human limitations. He doesn't get busy with someone else and forget us. He isn't exasperated and tired of hearing from us. He is always gracious and always there.

I love telling you stories about children around the world who discovered how God was there for them. I hope you were encouraged by the story of Gervens. I was encouraged to learn recently that his father is visiting him now regularly at the orphanage.

We don't know where his story will go, but I love how one day when he looks back over his life, he will know for sure that he was never left alone. God was always with him.

It's important for me to remember that being always in the presence or protection of God doesn't mean hard things can't happen to us. Mario and Daniela are examples of children whom God walked alongside as they faced illness and pain. He's on every page of our stories—the really great ones and the pretty desperate ones. He hurts when we do, and he rejoices with us. He is using all circumstances to reveal himself to us and grow us up.

We can talk to him throughout each day, knowing he is ever-present in every story.

This last year my husband, Todd, and I took a trip to Israel and Turkey with a Bible teacher named Ray Vanderlaan. What's called Turkey today used to be called Asia Minor, and it's where the very earliest Christian churches were planted. I went there expecting to learn truths about biblical characters and the context in which their stories took place. I came home understanding more about how *my* story is engaged in a mission thousands of years old. (And so is yours . . .)

Throughout the Bible, God calls us to be his priests and together we make up what's called a kingdom of priests. First Peter 2:9 says, "You are . . . a royal priesthood." So what then is a priest's mission?

To show others what God is like.

That's why we meet human needs, to show someone what God is like. It's why we pray for someone, or reach out to others. We are showing someone who might not otherwise see or know God—this is what he looks like. Annita showed Daniela; the kids in the youth group showed Happy and her village friends. When we show others what God is like, big stories start to unfold before us. Every day, every time you share your snack, or sit with someone who doesn't have someone to be with, or help a brother or sister with homework, you are showing them what God is like.

This expands God's kingdom.

It's been a challenge for me to consider this biblical truth since I've been back

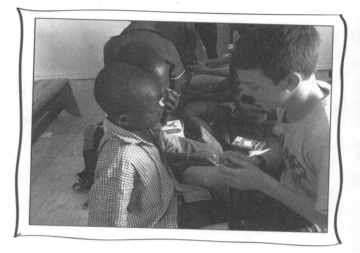

from my trip. I keep thinking of how I can put-God-on-display when things are hard or I am angry or afraid. In those moments, if I choose to show God's light, it's evidence to others he's *real*. Being a priest means I am more than just the *recipient* of God's goodness, mercy, forgiveness, gifts, and grace. Being a priest means I am a *channel* of his goodness, mercy, forgiveness, gifts, and grace to others. Wow!

A priest is a servant who puts his own needs last. I am tested in this, as I want to naturally go first in line and make myself the most comfortable. I have to put that natural self to death in order for someone to see the supernatural at work in me and then wonder less about Beth and more about Jesus. All this is about having our hands open and being engaged in God's business. All the stories I've shared about children around the world include people who acted like Jesus to children who desperately needed to see that he still cared.

Being engaged in God's business takes a lot of prayer and can grow you up fast. Since our newly adopted seventh-grade son has been home these last few months from Mexico, I have wrestled with being everything Tyler needs me to be. How can I be patient, when patience is running out, or wise, when I'm not sure what to do? How can I be loving or peaceful or joyful in *any* circumstance, and not just the easy ones?

There's only one way.

I have to go to Jesus to fill my cup. He will give me every day exactly what I need for this holy assignment (and all the others). This morning, I was thinking, *How do I get him ready for school? How do I point out to him what needs adjusting for his assimilation into American junior high?* In those moments, I was focusing too much on what he wasn't, instead of what he was. I felt convicted when I later read these words of Jesus:

Don't pick on people, jump on their failures, criticize their faults—unless, of course, you want the same treatment. That critical spirit has a way of boomeranging. . . . Here is a simple, rule-of-thumb guide for behavior: Ask yourself what you want people to do for you, then grab the initiative and do it for *them* (Matthew 7:1, 2, 12, *The Message*).

Tyler just wants to be loved. The kid in your school cafeteria or on your soccer team or on your bus just wants to be loved. We can spend a lot of time focused on good activities, but miss what God is asking from us on any given day.

Just love others, in my name.

I don't want any critical spirit boomeranging back to me, and I don't want to wait until someone does or doesn't do what I hope they will. I want to ask myself what it is I want people to do for me, and instead, take the initiative toward them. I am hoping then my behavior will say loud and clear, "God loves you." In this way, I am acting like God's representative on earth.

This is what Tanya's mom did when she opened her life to a new girl from Ukraine and walked into a big story. She needed more than what she had in herself, and so she asked God to fill her up. The end result is more than just a mother-daughter relationship, it's the creation of a family. God is multifaceted like that. He blesses Tanya, he blesses Andra and Travis, her parents, he blesses Tanya's new friends, and all of us who hear her story. When we say yes to

God's leading, he tells great truths through our lives.

Annita did the same when she invested in Daniela. She needed patience and wisdom, grace and mercy—all in measures more than she had naturally. She asked God to show himself through her. And as a result, God began to heal body and spirit in Daniela, and her story continues.

I am confident of what God will do through you when you show others what he is like. I believe he'll tell his story through your life as you love the kids in your neighborhood and around the world. When we reach out to others, and pray for them, or give to them, or share our lives with them, we end up being blessed, and can forget whether we are the giver or the receiver. As we reach out in his name, we connect with others and soon will find ourselves surrounded by his stories. It's how he shows us we are not alone. He is sending his community to surround you with his love, and then he'll send you to come alongside others.

This is God's way. Join him!

Beth wrote her first book in third grade. It was about a frog. Mrs. Pate may never have liked it, but her mother still takes it out and looks at it occasionally. Since then, Beth has written other books, such as *Reckless Faith* (Zondervan, 2008), *Relentless*

Hope (Standard Publishing, 2011), *Tales of the Not Forgotten* (Standard Publishing, 2012), *Tales of the Defended Ones* (Standard Publishing, 2013), *Tales of the Ones Led Out* (Standard Publishing, 2014), and *Tales of the Ones He Won't Let Go* (Standard Publishing, 2014).

Beth has a houseful of kids—there are some in elementary, a couple in junior high, a high-schooler, a few college students, and two who live independently now. Besides her family, Beth likes all forms of chocolate, the ocean in any season, traveling, and Christmastime.

Beth met her husband, Todd, at age seventeen at Young Life Bible study. She knew she liked him when he offered her one of his three versions of the Bible (since she had forgotten hers). Together they have spent seventeen years on the mission field and continue to work together with Back2Back Ministries to bring care for today and hope for tomorrow to orphans around the world.

Acknowledgments

It takes a lot to get a book in print, so thank you to the whole Standard Publishing team—you have each played a part in the success of the Storyweaver series. Thank you for allowing me to continue to put these stories out there for the next generation.

Thank you to Lauren Neal, for sharing so well Gervens's story. I am always praying for your missionary journey. Thank you to Mario, for vulnerably being willing to share what family reconciliation can look like. Thank you to Tanya's family. I wept the first time I heard your story and still get misty-eyed with each retelling. I hope you live fully in your story line. Thank you also to Andrea for supplying such detail. Thank you to Anna Valdez and Daniela for allowing a glimpse into your Christmas miracle and into the testimony still unfolding. Thank you to Leah Smart and Jason Munafo for supplying details on Happy and this Nigerian miracle.

Thank you to my family—you know all the ways you join in on this life. I couldn't be prouder of each of you for the ways you listen to the Storyweaver.

Thank you, Todd, for always listening, supporting, and trusting that these words are part of a bigger plan. I can't imagine this family or this life without you.

Learn More

Would you like to learn more about being a missionary or about some of the organizations listed in this book? Go online (or ask for permission to go online) or write for information to learn more about some of the organizations that are helping kids in the United States, Ukraine, Mexico, Haiti, Nigeria, and all over the world!

Back2Back Ministries
P.O. Box 70
Mason, OH 45050
www.back2back.org

New Horizons for Children
5330 Brookstone Dr., Suite 250
P.O. Box 801395
Acworth, GA 30101
www.nhfc.org

Jesus in Haiti Ministries

c/o Hartley Tax & Accounting LLC

6066 E State Blvd.

Fort Wayne, IN 46815

www.jesusinhaiti.org

The Storyweaver Series

How is God weaving your story?

These powerful stories of God's work in the lives of poor and abandoned kids will inspire the kids in your class to get involved in missions.

Beth Guckenberger, Co-Executive Director of Back2Back Ministries, shares a collection of unforgettable, real stories in each of these books. Spark an interest in your students to consider God as their Storyweaver and to wonder about a world bigger than the one they know.

BACK2BACK
MINISTRIES

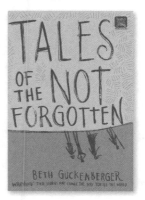

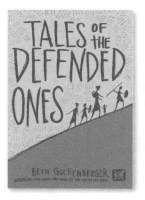

Tales of the Not Forgotten
Item #: 025485212
ISBN: 978-0-7847-3528-2
Price: $8.99

Tales of the Defended Ones
Item #: 025495113
ISBN: 978-0-7847-3697-5
Price: $8.99

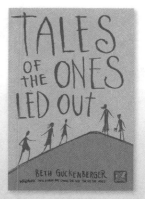

"Stories are so extremely powerful, and the ones in this book will absolutely rock your world!"
Ryan Frank, KidzMatter

Tales of the Ones Led Out
Item #: 025611414
ISBN: 978-0-7847-7522-6
Price: $8.99

Tales of the Ones He Won't Let Go
Item #: 025611614
ISBN: 978-0-7847-7634-6
Price: $8.99

Kids Serving Kids

Help kids develop a heart for helping others.

Filled with fun, interactive learning experiences, biblical teaching, and kid-inspired service projects, this missions curriculum will open kids' eyes to the needs in their community and around the world—then challenge them to do something about it!

Each Super Simple Mission Kit includes:

- An easy-to-use Director's Guide
- A DVD with complete customizable materials for six lessons—includes videos, worship music by Yancy, and more
- A Tales of the Not Forgotten or Tales of the Ones He Won't Let Go book, which serves as the basis for the 6-lesson curriculum—additional copies can be purchased for your kids and leaders
- Missions posters

**Fully Resourced
Missions Curriculum**

Your purchase of these kits supports orphan care worldwide.

Great as a:
- **Curriculum for your church missions conference**
- **Follow-up or alternative to VBS**
- **Missions experience during school breaks**
- **Family ministry event**
- **Midweek or Sunday school program**

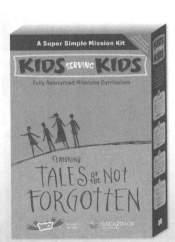

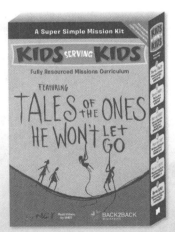

Kids Serving Kids™ Super Simple Mission Kit featuring Tales of the Not Forgotten

Item #: 025610913
ISBN: 978-0-7847-7479-3
Price: $49.99

Kids Serving Kids™ Super Simple Mission Kit featuring Tales of the Ones He Won't Let Go

Item #: 025611814
ISBN: 978-0-7847-7635-3
Price: $49.99

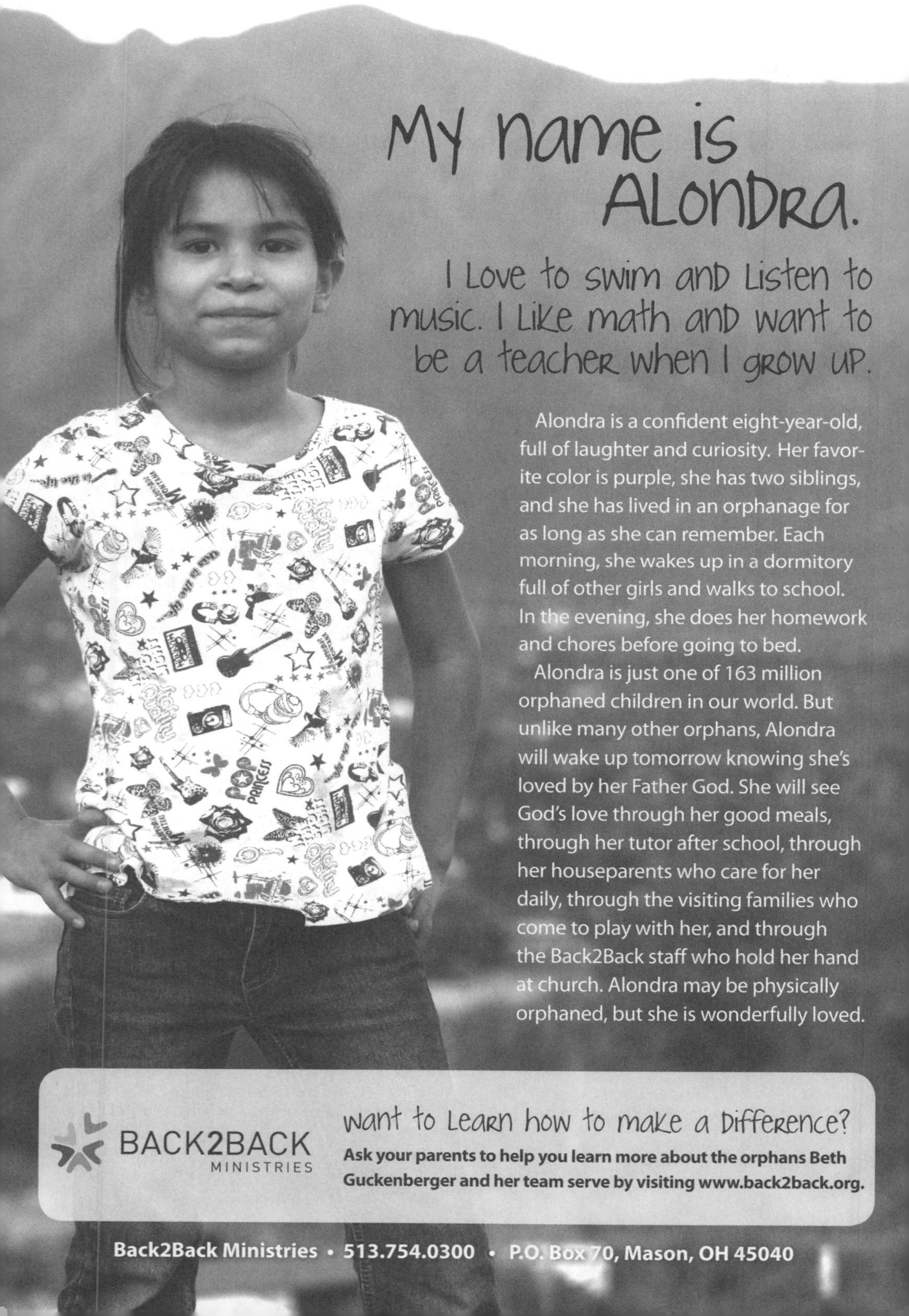
My name is Alondra.
I love to swim and listen to music. I like math and want to be a teacher when I grow up.
Alondra is a confident eight-year-old, full of laughter and curiosity. Her favorite color is purple, she has two siblings, and she has lived in an orphanage for as long as she can remember. Each morning, she wakes up in a dormitory full of other girls and walks to school. In the evening, she does her homework and chores before going to bed.
Alondra is just one of 163 million orphaned children in our world. But unlike many other orphans, Alondra will wake up tomorrow knowing she's loved by her Father God. She will see God's love through her good meals, through her tutor after school, through her houseparents who care for her daily, through the visiting families who come to play with her, and through the Back2Back staff who hold her hand at church. Alondra may be physically orphaned, but she is wonderfully loved.
BACK2BACK MINISTRIES
Want to learn how to make a difference?
Ask your parents to help you learn more about the orphans Beth Guckenberger and her team serve by visiting www.back2back.org.
Back2Back Ministries • 513.754.0300 • P.O. Box 70, Mason, OH 45040

My name is Daniel.

I like to play soccer and climb the rocks behind my house. My favorite subject is English.

Daniel lives in Jos, Nigeria, where he attends Back2Back's Education Center. At the center, he has good meals, care when he is sick, and a safe place to learn.

When Daniel first came to the Education Center, he was very shy. He rarely laughed or smiled. But now, through the love and attention of Back2Back staff, he has grown to become a confident boy, full of laughter and joy.

Daniel hopes to be a teacher when he grows up. For the first time in his life, Daniel is thriving and well on his way to reaching his goals for a brighter tomorrow.

BACK2BACK
MINISTRIES

want to Learn how to make a Difference?
Ask your parents to help you learn more about the orphans Beth Guckenberger and her team serve by visiting www.back2back.org.

Back2Back Ministries • 513.754.0300 • P.O. Box 70, Mason, OH 45040

Living in a children's home, Daniela couldn't control much. But she could certainly control how she moved, until one day . . .

"Help! I can't walk!"

Daniela receives healing for unknown wounds. Gervens brings light out of dark places. Happy discovers strength in new words. Tanya travels far to come home. Mario lets go and reaches for his future.

Their languages and locations may be different from yours, but our hearts are all united by the promises made by our great Storyweaver God—our Guide, who leads us into adventures we couldn't dream of and travels we might never have signed up for on our own. Follow the paths of these five young men and women as they discover the God who never leaves us, the God who faithfully writes every chapter of the . . .

TALES OF THE NEVER ALONE

JUVENILE FICTION / Religious / Christian / Social Issue
RELIGION / Religious / Christian Life / Inspiration

ISBN 978-0-7847-7769-5

Standard® PUBLISHING
www.standardpub.com

STORYWEAVER

9 780784 777695
025626315   Ages 8 & U